INDIAN

INDIAN SUMMER

Pauline Bracken

Pauline Bracken (signature)

THE COLLINS PRESS

To my husband, Niall

Published by The Collins Press, Carey's Lane, The Huguenot
Quarter, Cork 1997

Printed in Ireland by Colour Books Ltd., Dublin

Cover design by Upper Case Ltd., Cornmarket Street, Cork
Cover painting by Vicky Wilson

ISBN: 1-898256-22-5

1

IT WAS on Keel Strand, on Achill Island, off the coast of County Mayo in Ireland that the young man first saw a girl running along the edge of the water, her ankles lapped by the surf, and instantly lost his heart to her. Keel would become their strand, the beach where they would walk, run, lie in the sun and come to terms with the knowledge that everything that has been expressed about human love can be said to be true, but that it is unique each time it happens between two people.

The girl was but eighteen years of age, with thick, black, wavy hair, deep blue eyes and a pale and perfect skin. Her beautiful face and fine lithe body were pure magic to the man, and she, in turn, was overwhelmed by his power of attraction for her. He too was dark-haired with hazel eyes and a handsome face, boasting a well-built figure befitting a man of twenty-two. As an art student he drank in the colours around him in Achill, but he was captivated most of all by the colour of the eyes of his lover and, walking along the beach, he would look into them and say, 'Run ahead along the edge of the water, the way you were when I first saw you from the cliff', and she would answer, 'Only if you kiss me first!' Sometimes she went ahead for quite some distance before stopping to sit down on the beach, and wait for him among the rocks, and when he re-joined her they would lie there, rejoicing in their love for one another.

They stayed in the local guest house where the man had a room in an annexe, and they spent the evenings in the pub where the music and 'craic' sprang into life once darkness fell. The man was often called upon to sing and the girl would watch him as if under a spell. Their companions teased them about their love affair, but left them in peace to enjoy it, and when everyone had dispersed, the young woman would steal out of her little room under the eaves, and tiptoe along the wooden corridor to go downstairs where she let herself out by the back door, into his waiting arms. He would open the door of the annexe while she slipped inside and then they would fall down onto the white cotton counterpane covering his bed, trying not to make noise and heaving with laughter and passion. The bed was narrow but it held them tightly together, and as her cotton nightdress slipped from her brown shoulders and he ran his finger tips over her sweet-smelling skin, her body would respond to his and their love-making would become a third and ruling force. The lovers would receive new energy from their desire for one another and when their passion was at last spent, they would sleep briefly in the pale but growing light of a west of Ireland dawn. The light has a strange quality here in Achill, as if many shades of white and blue shimmer in it together, and as the girl started her return journey through the back door and up to her little room, the sun would come sliding over the sea, so that she would be grateful for the window blind which would conceal it while she slept soundly for a few hours.

Day after day they explored the island, sometimes digging for amethysts in the sandy cliff above Keem Bay, and one day the man presented his love with a fine purple stone which he had unearthed from the bank and said, 'I'll have a ring made for you from this and I'll wed you one day soon'. Other days they would go mountain-climbing on Croghan mountain, or walk along Lough Corrymore, looking across the waters which were said to be the place where the legendary Children of Lir had lived out their exile. The day they climbed Minawn mountain, they were rewarded with a fine view of Clew Bay, with a mauve-coloured Clare Island guarding its entrance, and they vowed to one another that they would return one day and renew their experience of its beauty and their own. Looking across the Atlantic they joked about New York being the next parish, and the man said he

6

would bring her there one day and show her the new world. She could see her whole life opening up before her like a Japanese flower in water, and he saw the world as his to give her.

The spring sunshine lit up the charming bedroom, furnished in biscuit and moss-green and white, and on her thirty-sixth birthday Dorothy Reynolds sat on the side of her bed and said to herself: I'm thirty-six today and I'm taking full control of my life. From now on I will lead my life on my own terms, I will decide whether or not whatever I am doing is right, and what is important. I'm thirty-six and I'm not sorry that I am.

A wave of confidence passed over her as she did a quick mental survey of her holdings:

Single, attractive, excellent health, good company with both men and women, an interesting job as an executive in a large advertising and Public Relations agency, all social entitlements intact and policies paid up, life membership of the small badminton club she had developed and modernised over the years with others, and still fancy-free as regards the men in her life. She had travelled a good deal and was happy to make her life in Ireland. She pulled on a white towelling wrap and strolled into the champagne-coloured ensuite bathroom to run the bath water. She would think out the remainder of her life's inventory while she was taking a bath, for she always had her best ideas when she was lying up to her neck in hot fragrant suds.

Dorothy Reynolds was a beautiful woman, with deep blue eyes and thick, black, wavy hair, an Irish colour-combination. Nearly everyone liked her and she was greatly admired by men, who enjoyed trying to break down her reserve while she enjoyed resisting their efforts. She had an excellent sense of the comic element in life and was popular at the badminton club or wherever she went socially. She liked to date, but never seemed interested in a permanent relationship.

Dorothy had a secret, so firmly closed away in her emotions that she had had to build her life apart from this event. At nineteen, she had borne a child, a little boy, and she had given him up for adoption. The only person who knew about it was her friend, Kate O'Grady.

Dorothy had not intended to tell Kate about the baby when they had become friends, but it had come out after about a year. They had met in the badminton club and had communicated like sisters, but the most important point in their friendship had been the evening they had casually gone to see a feature film. The film was followed by a short and powerful documentary about the trauma suffered by a woman who had given up a baby for adoption at nineteen years of age, and, set in the Ireland of twenty years earlier, it had followed the situation from the young mother's point of view. Kate had sat back and enjoyed both films, and when they emerged into the daylight she was amazed at the change in her friend. Dorothy's swollen eyes told their own tale.

'There's something terribly wrong, isn't there?' Kate had asked her. Dorothy could only nod. 'A quick cup of coffee somewhere. We'll slip into a pub and sit in a quiet corner and you'll just have to tell me all about it, whatever it is. I only hope you haven't murdered someone!' Usually the one to take the initiative, Dorothy had allowed herself to be led into a nearby pub where they had tucked themselves into a dark corner, Dorothy wiping her eyes while Kate offered coffee, afraid to order a drink in case it might upset Dorothy further, as she was already carried away on a wave of emotion

'Now, take a few sips. Settle down and tell me all. What upset you? Was it one of the films, the second one? I found it very moving too.'

'Yes, it was the second one ... Kate, I had a baby at the same age as that girl, and I too gave him up for adoption. I

8

didn't think I had any choice at the time ... I didn't want to tell my parents, and it would have hurt my aunt and uncle dreadfully. It all seems so foolish now, to have put everyone else before the baby, my own little baby, but I had no way of supporting it and I was rushed into the adoption in various ways ... The climate about babies outside wedlock was so different then ... Do you know, Kate, I've never got over it.'

'No, I don't suppose any woman really does. But ... what about the father? Didn't he come into it?'

'I vanished on him. He was so young, twenty-two and a student, that I couldn't face telling him. You see, we met on a holiday in Achill and fell wildly in love. I can hardly bear to think back on it, because I never met anyone like him since, and now, he has a son somewhere and doesn't know it.' Dorothy took a sip of coffee and wiped away another tear. 'What a mess I made of my life back then.'

'Stop talking as if you were ninety-nine,' said Kate and smiled kindly at her. 'Come on, Dorothy, tell me the next part of the story.'

'Well, I asked my aunt if I could go to London to do a business course, as that was the thing to do if you weren't going to college, and she was good enough to help me financially until an entitlement came through for me when I was twenty-one. I had the baby in London and he was adopted there. It was that film that brought it all back to me in a rush. I didn't quite realise how vulnerable I still am.'

'Don't be hard on yourself, Dorothy. Times were different then and you must have suffered a great deal, especially since you didn't confide in anyone.'

'I sealed up my emotions when it was over, Kate. I just had to get on with my life, and I've never felt able to tell anybody about it until now. But I know one thing for sure – it has come between me and forming any lasting relationship, although I've had lots of boyfriends down the years.'

'Was there no one in particular?'

'Once or twice I nearly took the ring, as I thought I was

fond enough of the man to settle down with him, but each time I found I couldn't. There you are, I'm an emotional cripple and it's my best kept secret.'

'You never heard anything further from the boy?'

'I never looked for him, as I thought I would probably spoil his life by walking into it, even if I did manage to find him.'

'People can have terrible regrets, to no purpose, and life isn't made for regrets, Dorothy. You know, you might take a bit of counselling sometime, if you find you're still unhappy in that area. I can tell you one thing – you would never know that Dorothy Reynolds carried a painful secret, and well done on that score.'

'The baby was collected by his adoptive parents when he was a week old, and I resolved never to tell anyone and to go out and make my life on my own. Maybe I made too good a job of it.'

'The boy would be around eighteen now, wouldn't he?' asked Kate, feeling that she wanted to make him a reality, now that she had the opportunity. Perhaps it would be more healing that way for Dorothy. 'He has his life, and you have yours. Live your life now and finish with regrets. I won't be telling anyone, not even Bill. This goes on ice, believe me.'

'Thank you, dear, dear Kate. I'm feeling a bit better now and some day I'll tell you details of my great love – some day, maybe.'

'Some day, Dorothy. No hurry, and not today, certainly.'

They had set off down town together, heads bent against the light rain.

'You're a good friend, Kate.'

'You're a good friend, yourself, Dorothy.' They parted then and they never discussed the matter again, although the friendship flourished.

Born to parents who had married late, Dorothy had been an only child, and when she was three years of age, her parents

10

had separated, her father returning to farm in Kenya, and her mother going to work in the United States as an actress. Their different aspirations had made the marriage impossible, once their initial infatuation had worn off. Dorothy had been born in Kenya and her mother had brought her back to Ireland, leaving her with her married sister, and departing to start a new life in America. Although she had returned to Ireland from time to time, to see her daughter, and Dorothy had visited her in the States during her teens, the aunt who had reared Dorothy had taken the place of her mother, and her mother the place of an aunt. She had not been unhappy growing up, just wistful that she couldn't be part of her parents' lives, and she had not lacked love, being brought up as a cherished child. All the same, emphasis had been laid on Dorothy pursuing an independent life and she had been well-educated. When she had expressed a wish to go into an advertising agency rather than to university, her aunt and uncle had thought it better to let her join the mainstream of life, as she wanted to do. 'I can always do a degree later on,' Dorothy had said, to console them, 'but just let me out into life. I'm longing for it.' And so it was that she had done a business course, and joined a leading advertising and public relations firm. While Dorothy was growing up she had erected a shell around herself emotionally, as although she loved her aunt, she missed having natural parents. She played a great deal of tennis and, later, badminton and she regarded herself as a 'loner', someone who would always be an observer of life, rather than be in the thick of it. Her close friendship with Kate had contributed greatly to her sense of self-worth.

Now at the ripe old age of thirty-six, it was time to make a career change

She lay back in the bath to think out her next move. How about taking up the recently offered severance package and accepting a good lump sum, forfeiting her salary, and going into public relations on her own? She had all the necessary

11

qualifications and experience, and she knew herself to be an excellent organiser. Her boss Brian Nolan had just retired and rather than join a new team, it was time to move on. Brian, who had been Director of Public Relations, had seen to it that she was well paid, but had kept her back over the years, frequently praising her work, but to the wrong people, as he had feared losing her, knowing how much he depended on her efficiency. They had worked closely and well for the firm, but Dorothy knew he viewed women with suspicion, particularly single women, when it came to promotion. Dorothy felt it was time to break with company loyalty, security and comfort.

'Dorothy Reynolds and Associates' sounded good. She lounged in the bath and said it aloud a few times. She could start by putting advertisements in business journals and leading newspapers, and might consider getting a partner for a budding PR business. Her town house at Sandymount in Dublin would be suitable as office premises, and once a computer, modem, fax and other office machines were installed, a client list compiled and secretarial help arranged, she would surely make a go of it. She had often been asked in the course of various promotions whether she would do a public relations project privately, but always refused if the work originated through the agency. All going well, a business of her own would take about two years to break even, and she could take on staff if business dictated the need. An accountant would be necessary from the start.

Dorothy felt a tingle of excitement as her mind roved across the project and she towelled herself dry, dressed in a suit of a pastel shade of linen and went out to investigate her newly structured future. First she would have a good chat with Kate.

'Meet me for lunch, Kate,' said Dorothy on the telephone, 'I have news for you. Not to be discussed over the phone, mind you, but I think you'll like it.'

'Lots of mystery,' said Kate, 'but that'll make for an

interesting lunch. Let's have fresh pasta and a glass of Chianti, and I'll be sitting on hot cakes to hear whatever it is.'

Kate O'Grady loved her husband Bill, her two teenage daughters and her part-time job in the bank. She worked from eleven to three every day although pulling back to half-day work had blighted her chances of promotion. She was gifted with figures, but she was of an easy-going disposition and had put the family before the career, not expecting to win on all sides of life, and settling for enjoying to the full what she had in hand.

Dyslexic to a degree, she did not retain how some words were spelt, or even their shape, and admirers of James Joyce would have enjoyed how she often, quite unconcernedly, ran two expressions into one. This sometimes startled people, but in general it went unnoticed. She came out with such expressions as 'I don't intend to become a couch sofa', or 'that will send us down the slippery slide', or even 'there is something smelling in the rat of Denmark' – a remark that had brought down the house on one occasion. She would just open her grey eyes wide and stare out anyone who drew attention to her style of expression, and eventually people got used to her describing herself as 'buzzing around like a blue-tailed bee' or 'slopping around the house in bad humour'. Whenever she was short of a verb she made one up, such as 'I snootched over and found what I was looking for', or 'my mother gets into her car and jags down the road'. In Kate-speak people 'bore the blunt of things', 'branded together' and 'had a conflab about something'. When a colleague had a bereavement, Kate described her as 'going around morosed down to the ground'. 'There was a lot going under her cloak and dagger' had caused suppressed laughter and, mercifully, Kate had not seen Dorothy moaning with giggles into her handkerchief one day in the club, when she had described a club member as 'not knowing one end of a tennis ball from the other'. Kate had firm opinions, knew exactly what was going on everywhere and would have described herself as being a 'mind of information'.

When they arrived at the restaurant, the two women pulled up chairs and ordered lunch. Friends always take a nose dive into conversation and so they were off immediately.

'Out with it fast. I'm dying to know your great revelation.'

'Meet Dorothy Reynolds and Associates. I'm resigning from the agency to open my own PR practice. I've taken the decision and I hope to open in two months' time. The moment has come for Dorothy Reynolds to sally forth and make a killing for herself.'

Kate looked at her friend, and although Dorothy was smiling, she could see that she spoke in earnest.

'You'll throw up all security and march out into the market? Well, good for you, that's all I can say at this stage. I've half a mind to brand together with you, now that I think of it. When I think of my careful half-day job in the bank it makes me want to do something wild sometimes. Tell me more.'

'I have to sort it out first with the agency, and see what kind of a severance deal they'll offer me. Then I want to open a practice from home, with a view to organising activities for groups in the off-season in Irish hotels. It's not exactly tourism, but there is a cross-over.' On and on they talked and by the time they had consumed some good Italian pasta and wine, they had crossed all the 't's and dotted the 'i's.

The following week Dorothy outlined her plans to the agency. The personnel people were shocked that she should think of going, as she suited the work so well, and some days later she received a calculation of a severance package, which came as a pleasant surprise. She kept her plans a secret at work and did not even tell her steady man, Stephen Jackson, who came to town regularly from Northern Ireland and was constantly trying to get her to marry him. Dorothy

14

suddenly went around feeling she owned the world, thinking out her new life. It felt good to be healthy, independent, solvent, ambitious – and thirty-six.

Shortly after Brian Nolan retired at sixty from the advertising agency where he had worked all his life, he dropped in to collect some reference books he had been using regularly. His send-off had been pleasant enough, and people had said good things about his forty years' service. There had been the usual joshing about his being busier than ever now that he was retiring, and the presentation of the latest fax and telephone answering machine on the market had looked good in everyone's eyes. In fact he had been asked in advance what he would like as a gift, and once he knew the amount of the collection, his suggestion of a fax had saved him buying one for himself. Brian liked presents which saved him money, and the new machine had given his study at home a look of 'full steam ahead' when he had placed it on his inherited mahogany desk. Now he was limbering up to start a new chapter in life after so many years in an organisation, and he was feeling optimistic as he crossed the reception area and swung down the corridor to 'his' office. He tapped lightly on the door, feeling amused at the gesture, turned the handle and walked into the room with the brisk movements of a small man who has had to rely on an air of purpose to effect presence.

'Brian, eh, hello, how *are* you?' said the newly-appointed Director of Public Relations, Tom Bates, from behind the desk Brian had sat at only a few days previously. Bates was a little taken aback by the visit, but he covered up smilingly and said, 'You're looking great. Off to play golf I suppose, are you?'

Instantly, Brian felt patronised. Tom Bates had been his subordinate.

'I don't suppose I look any different to a few days ago,' he said brightly, if a little coldly, 'and I don't play golf, as it happens. Do you?'

'Oh, I forgot you don't. There's nothing I like better than a game at the weekend. You might find yourself taking it up, now that you have more time on your hands.'

Brian didn't answer. Instead, he crossed the floor to the book shelves and began to take down volumes.

'These are mine,' he said briefly over his shoulder. 'I'll be needing them, so I've dropped in for them.' He took down the current *Institute of Public Administration Year Book and Diary*. 'I'll need this too,' he said.

Tom watched him as he busied himself at the book shelves.

'No, Brian. I'll need that diary. It goes with the job, you see, as do most of the other directories.' As he spoke he looked across at the books in Brian's hands. Brian stiffened.

'The *IPA Diary* is for my use. I've made entries in it already, which I'll need.'

Tom didn't push the point and Brian went on scanning the shelves and picking out reference books. 'Just as long as you let me know the ones you've taken,' said Tom agreeably, deciding to back down, but making his point all the same.

Brian nodded in a non-commital way and after a few further minutes he gathered up the books and left without reference to them saying, 'See you here and there, I suppose.' His stomach churned as he walked back down the stairs and he didn't recognise the woman coming towards him.

'Brian ... you're looking very well indeed,' she said as they drew level. 'What are you up to? I thought you'd be far and away by now, playing golf or the like. How *are* you anyway?'

It was Rita, secretary to the Chairman, and someone he had often chatted to at meetings.

'I'm fine, Rita. Dropped in to collect a few things. How are *you*?'

He switched the conversation away from himself.

'Oh, the same as yesterday, today and tomorrow,' said

Rita, laughing. 'Nothing changes around here, sure it does-n't?'

'Good to see you, Rita, we'll talk again, I'm dashing.' He gave her an over-lively grin and continued towards the reception area. He felt awful. He hurried across the thickly carpeted floor and passed the Chairman in conversation with a smartly dressed man. Neither of them saw him as their heads were turned towards one another. Brian hurried out the front door and stood on the steps for a few moments, letting the air brush his face lightly. He was struck with the realisation that it didn't matter whether he turned left or right. He wasn't going to an appointment in either direction. Instead he crossed against the traffic, making a car pull up suddenly, and strode down a side street, moving fast and going nowhere.

Brian Nolan was not a particularly pleasant man, although he had got on well in business life. He knew his own failings and had gone through the years *not* trying to be agreeable, and using this stance as a means of getting and holding on to whatever he wanted at any time. Having a good brain, and being well-educated, he had risen in the agency by fending off competition, safe in the knowledge that he hadn't given anyone the feeling that they could appeal to him, and commanding respect by the quality of his work rather than through inter-personal relationships.

Crossed in love in his mid-twenties when he had relent-lessly pursued a girl who didn't want him, Brian had waited until he was forty to ask someone to marry him. He had found a strong, independent Irish woman who was working as a researcher in Wales, and who was home on holidays. She had been ready to settle down when he proposed to her, after inviting her out to dinner two nights running. She had accepted his offer and they married a couple of months later.

Brian had surprised himself and anyone who knew him by turning out to be a very good husband, and, in due course, an excellent father to their two sons. The house, marriage and boys were part of his lifestyle and he felt suitably fulfilled between family and work. He hadn't expected to feel wildly happy in his marriage and was very glad to enjoy a contented family life. He had given his wife, Vera, plenty of freedom and he had not minded how she spent her time, or how she furnished the house, as long as it was inexpensively and comfortably done, and when she had trained as a career guidance counsellor to take up part-time work once the boys were sufficiently reared, that was all right with him too. He wasn't exactly mean about housekeeping money but he preferred to give his wife a cheque or use a credit card rather than hand her cash, as he felt that giving actual money signified loss of control in his area.

Brian was now marching down Fleet Street, the books unwrapped under his arm, as if going from one office to another. He suddenly felt that the volumes would be better covered, in case he met any former colleagues in the area, and he wheeled into a delicatessen to make a random purchase in order to get a carrier bag.

'Mr Nolan, how *are* you?' said a loud voice in his ear, as he went to pay for a Brie cheese. He looked up sharply to see one of the trainee executives from the agency beside him with wrapped up sandwiches in his hand. 'You're looking fine, I must say. Enjoying your retirement?'

Brian nodded and rather than snap at the fellow he said, 'Yes, yes, indeed.' He breathed quickly down his nose to gain composure and made a sound like a snort, which he covered up with a cough.

'Nice assortment of cheese they have here,' he said pleasantly.

'I only come in for sandwiches or filled rolls for lunch at the desk,' the young man said. Just as Brian was going to compose some answer he was deflected by a cashier reaching out for the purchase and he gratefully got involved in the transaction.

'See you around, Mr Nolan. That's unless you're off fish-

18

ing every day!' and the young man paid exact money for his sandwich and breezed out of the shop with the quality of youth. Brian smiled bleakly in acknowledgement and turned back to ask the cashier for a larger carrier bag. He put the books and cheese into it and set off to walk the three miles to his home.

Brian intended to open a business consultancy of his own. On setting out that morning he had planned to visit the bookshops in the Dawson Street area of Dublin and see what was selling well in that line, but in his present confusion he was some distance out of town when he remembered. So this was retirement? A man scurrying home with cheese and some pirated directories concealed in a carrier bag! A light panic assailed him, but he recognised it as such and shook it off. This is sheer nonsense, he said to himself severely as he walked along. The answer is to get down to work immediately.

At home that afternoon Brian stayed devotedly at his desk, not even getting up to make a cup of tea. He listed the companies he wanted to approach about his consultancy and he was so busy working that he forgot to put on his desk light, until darkness almost enveloped him. He was used to managing his own work and had not been influenced by colleagues, so he had thought out his plans for a consultancy on his own, fully believing that the many contacts he had made while in the company would lead to valuable work opportunities. As he worked, the encounters of that morning became an unpleasant memory, and eventually he banished them from his mind. Tomorrow would be the real start of his new life.

Vera Nolan came in from her job as a career counsellor in a secondary school and set about putting the evening meal together, once she had looked in on her husband in his study.

'I'll call you when I have the dinner ready,' she said and

waved from the door.

Fifty-three years of age and seven years younger than Brian, she regarded herself as having been dealt quite a good hand of cards in life. She knew herself well and recognised the core of aggression in her personality, which had never been sufficiently challenged by hardship to have it broken, and she had an in-built determination to win in small matters, which can be as destructive as it can be an asset. She didn't actually like herself as a person, but she admired herself tremendously and was proud of her own single-mindedness, strong survival instinct and capacity to give life and nurture other creatures as long as she could dominate them.

Vera had married in her early thirties, assuming that she would make a go of it and that she would have children. She had produced two boys who were now nineteen and eighteen, respectively, and both were at university and resident in their colleges. Maternal in that she was a good reliable mother, she sneakingly regarded her sons, Ben and Jack, as among her accomplishments, and down the years had been tiresome in company, speaking about them as though they were quite superior to other young people, which they were not. If she were feeling bored in company, she did this to discountenance those forced to listen to her.

About five feet eight in height, Vera had firm features with a lovely straight nose, and she always had her thick short brown hair cut by an expensive stylist. She wasn't interested in make-up and merely applied moisturisers to keep her skin fresh, and a trace of lipstick when going out. She found this enabled her to giggle at make-up on others if she wanted to. She was taller than her husband and had a good carriage, but she tended to wear rather dull clothes, featuring maroon, rust, moss-green and black, and usually wearing them in combination, preferring to draw attention to herself physically by exuding a measure of power. People tended to consult her about their preoccupations and ask her advice, often when she knew less than they did about the subject in hand. She had been drawn to career counselling for its position of authority, and she did the job reasonably well, but the young people who came to her for help went away again, armed with addresses and advice but without self-confidence, as there was no real interest, affection or compassion in her dealings with them.

When Vera reached college-going age, it was with the aim of getting a degree rather than acquiring knowledge for its own sake that she had gone to university, and when she left, her mind was exactly as broad as it had been when going in at eighteen. She had worked as a researcher, first in Dublin, then in London and later in Wales, but she had been singularly disinterested in reading, regarding herself as having a well-paid and regular job, which gave her the means to pursue an independent life. When she married Brian, she gave up work outside the home and concentrated on rearing the two boys, and although she and Brian had entertained quite a lot as a pair on the dinner party circuit, Vera had plenty of acquaintances but no real friends. She liked to absorb information from other people, not befriend them, and she had a puzzling way of carrying on an animated conversation which, although it appeared to be friendly, was more often a vacuuming process for whatever was of interest to her. No one would ever have regarded her as lazy, but she aimed to get through life expending a minimum of effort on others. At home, Vera had always felt impregnable, and when she took up studying for career counselling, her approach had been characteristically narrow.

2

THIS EVENING, Vera busied herself about the kitchen. She liked cooking and enjoyed putting an inexpensive and cleverly devised meal on the table. She energetically kept the freezer stocked with good plain food, not thinking of preparing a meal as troublesome, but just another part of living.

As a young woman, she had always been the taker rather the giver in relationships with men, and her few flings abroad had been indulged in mainly to gain experience, something she wouldn't do at home. Above all, she valued the control she had over her single life. She had been faithful in her marriage to Brian for two reasons: no one had appealed to her sufficiently to inconvenience herself to the point of involving herself with them, and anyway, Dublin was too close-knit socially for undetected extra-marital activity. Life was ticking along for her now, with the two boys reared, and she and Brian were back to a two-person household, entertaining occasionally, but not maintaining friendships of any depth.

Now as she started the meal, Vera chatted to Brian about her day and asked him how he had got on with his.

'It went fine,' he answered, having prepared a response to an issue which would obviously be raised. 'I did a few things about town and I dropped into the agency to collect some books I needed. Useful for research.'

'Did you meet anyone interesting?'

'Not really. I hadn't much time to spend there as I wanted to check on what's in the bookshops in my line, now that I'm setting up my consultancy.' Brian gave his perfectly done steak all his attention, and was relieved when Vera switched to a new topic.

'I'm joining a writers' group,' she said suddenly.

'A writers' group?' he repeated after her. 'What do you want to write about?' Vera was immediately irritated, knowing that Brian would make her feel silly if she told him of her idea, but still wanting to mention it, now that her mind was made up about it.

'Oh, anything I feel like writing about.'

'Do you want to become a journalist?'

'I was thinking rather of creative writing. I've often felt I'd like to write, and I'm doing something about it now.'

'Warn me when your blockbuster is coming out,' he said drily.

'Oh come on Brian, you've never written anything creative yourself, so you think no one else you know can,' she said and began to clear away the main course to signal that she was finishing the discussion. When she left the room and reappeared with the sweet, she went on to other topics featured in the television news and the newspapers.

Brian always reacted to new activities on her part by presuming that she was only taking up interests to impress other people, and he was partly right. Her colleagues would probably say to her: Vera, you make us all look like bus stops. Boundless energy! Wish I were like you.

Vera had avoided any form of creativity all her life because she was afraid of it, and had no talent for it; she had also been too bent on quantifiable accomplishment to have the confidence and patience to toil along the chequered road that leads to the Arts. Now she had reached a point where she was beginning to be fascinated by it, with the same draw that accounts for the plain beautician, the toneless musician and the timid public relations person. She felt down-graded by the creativity of others, but she visited art exhibitions, occasionally went to poetry readings and liked an odd visit to the theatre. Of late she had entertained a wish to produce something original herself, to be known as someone artistic or literary, and she felt that writing would be the most suitable type of creativity for her. Apart from the odd smart letter about something inconsequential to *The Irish Times*, she had never had anything printed, and she only wrote such letters so that people would mention them to her, and give her something to which she could react from higher ground. If there were no recipe, Vera couldn't produce the goods; if there were, maybe she could, and that was how she saw it. But now, with the strange rush of awareness that comes across people over fifty, that this is life and not just a dress rehearsal, Vera had applied to join a creative writers' class in one of Dublin's universities. It was an attempt to get rid of her feeling of lack of fulfilment in that area, and she intended to go through with it. She invested in a clipboard, some pads of lined paper, an up-to-date dictionary and a new pen. The class was to be held on one night a week and participation was limited to fifteen people.

On the first night, Vera went along with mixed feelings, determination combined with a sensation of not being in control of what she was doing, and a distinct awareness of her creative inadequacy. She hoped she wouldn't meet anyone she knew there, as she regarded writing as a form of baring the soul, and this was not her style.

Ten women and five men came into the room. Some nodded shyly, others affected aloofness and some sat down purposefully, with much spreading of notebooks and turning of pages of periodicals. Vera sat down beside a man who looked to be in his early forties, without seeing him properly, as she was concentrating on herself, and just exchanged a mumbled 'Good evening' with him. The lecturer began her introductory talk and Vera instinctively felt disappointment, finding that that indefinable element which ignites a creative spark in others was not there. This was what she had been looking for in coming to the course. Still, the others in the class seemed to be quite attentive, so she made herself concentrate alongside.

At the break she looked around. Her class mates included women in long sweaters and leggings, a few older women with worried faces, one or two elderly men with introverted expressions and two young girls, who spent the time exchanging glances and pulling woe-begone faces at one another. Vera sat back and relaxed.

'I'm not inspired as yet, are you?' It was the man beside her. Vera looked at him properly for the first time. Rather French looking, with hair *en brosse*, a good face with smiling brown eyes, and dressed in smart casual clothes.

'Eh, no I'm not, but it's only the first session, and maybe inspiration will strike.'

'Hopefully.'

'I'm here to learn, I suppose, so I can't expect to get ahead fast. Any time I've tried to write, I've felt that everything has been said about everything.'

'I've written a little, and I'm here to get back the drive to do some more, but I'm not hopeful so far. I'll give it a try.' He smiled at her attractively and then the lecturer took over again. The theme of an Irish heatwave was suggested as a short piece to be done at home for the following week, and the class broke up. The man smiled pleasantly as he got up to go and said, 'Back next week, I presume. Goodbye'. Vera wanted to talk to the lecturer on the way out, but found she was taken up with the two young girls, so she left the room feeling rather flat.

'Well, come up with anything startling?' It was Brian's greeting when she got home. 'One step nearer to producing something which will make you the toast of the town? I'm joking. How did it go?' Vera didn't usually take any notice of his chaffing about her activities, and tonight she didn't feel like sharing her thoughts.

'We're not allowed to tell others how we're thinking, so don't expect bulletins.'

'When did anyone ever tell you what you were allowed to think or do – since you were in a gym-slip, that is?' He was still scanning the newspaper he had been reading when she came in.

'Oh, give over,' Vera said casually and went out to the kitchen to put on the kettle for tea. At least she had done something about this writing business, and that was the main thing. She brought in the tea, poured it out for both of them and made herself comfortable, taking out a knitting bag and starting to count stitches according to a pattern. *The News* was coming up on television and she dismissed the evening from her mind.

When Vera left for work the following morning, Brian thought he would start his day with a walk on Sandymount Strand. This strand is on the south side of Dublin's horse-shoe bay, and the seafront can be reached easily and quickly from a number of districts, with a long seaboard stretching from Sandymount to Killiney on the south side, and from Clontarf to Howth on the north side. On the other side of the Howth peninsula, the same uncluttered scenery is offered by Portmarnock and Malahide, running on to other long stretches of beach at Donabate and further on. When Dubliners feel they need some space they either head for the seafront or turn their back on the bay and make for the hills, or 'Dublin Mountains', as they are known, a chain of hills running southward to reach the Wicklow Mountains.

Today Brian chose the seafront, where he felt he could think out his future more clearly, and he drove to Sandymount, parked his car and changed into rubber boots for walking on the sand, the same beach where James Joyce 'walked into eternity across Sandymount Strand'. The tide was out and he set out across the vast beach to the point where the water welled in from Blackrock, with Dun Laoghaire harbour sparkling in the distance. It was a cold, bright, early spring morning and he was dressed warmly, but somehow he felt unnaturally tired and a little cold. Still, it was a good time for a thinking session and a walk combined. The twin red and white striped chimneys of the Pigeon House power station stood out against the clear sky, and their two plumes of white smoke hung in parallel slants, unintentionally lending perspective to the flat landscape, apart from

26

Howth's soft, rounded head on the other side of the bay. A white ship edged its way very slowly out of the port of Dublin and Brian gazed at it for a few minutes, checking that it was actually moving. He contemplated Howth and wondered if it might be more pleasant to live on that side of the bay, and look across at the south city shore line. The idea of moving anywhere hadn't crossed his mind until now, and it was then that he fully realised that he hadn't thought his retirement through.

His mind switched to the previous day and his work at his desk at home. He had felt vaguely annoyed at the difficulty he had encountered in checking information from public offices, and he had been somewhat peremptory in his requests, thinking that information officers were not answering up in the manner that he, as a member of the public, was entitled to be replied to. In the agency, he had had Dorothy Reynolds to track down details for him, and now he found it extremely tiresome to have to do it for himself. 'Isn't it your job to know the answer to that?' he had enquired of one person, and when she had replied that it was her job to direct him in his enquiries, as she helped all callers, but not to do his research for him, he hadn't liked it at all. Brian had nearly huffed when it was suggested to him that he contact a commercial research service, such as that offered by *The Irish Times*, but he had realised that the officer was right and he was overdoing things. He would investigate the commercial computerised information services, and look over the bookshops. He had also annoyed himself by not knowing the cost of a postage stamp for an ordinary sealed envelope. Of course it was unimportant, but he had phoned the General Post Office to know rather than ask Vera, in case she brought it up for a laugh at a dinner party. Vera paid the bills and sent out Christmas cards and he had never had to stamp letters, but now he wondered what other small traps awaited him. Silly to even register such trivia, he told himself shortly. He walked across the strand and back, thinking out various aspects of his consultancy, and returned to his car to set off for home. Brian vowed to himself that he was going to make a success of the next part of his life.

Vera returned to the writers' group the following week, bringing along her piece of homework on an Irish heatwave, and how the Irish coped with such an unexpected treat. She regarded her efforts as pathetic. She also went along early, so that she could choose a place, and others coming in could sit near her or otherwise. Hardly admitting it to herself, Vera hoped that the man from last week would come in and sit down beside her, as he appeared to be the most interesting person in the group, and she liked to dominate at least one person in any situation where she might feel inadequate. She wore her good suede jacket, a fine cream polo-neck sweater which she had received as a present, but which she had never worn, and a pair of dark brown ski-type pants which she had bought at a recent sale. For some reason she had a desire to improve her appearance and she had a suspicion that it was not unconnected with the man in the class. She sniggered to herself at the idea, but going through the hall, on the way out, she thought she looked co-ordinated, and felt that the light leather briefcase made her look 'academic'.

Brian had been very quiet all week, apparently immersed in setting up his consultancy and she wondered whether he would make a success of it. As long as she was out of the house during the day at her job, it would be an asset to have him working at home. The incidence of burglary in Dublin had been increasing and one never knew who would be next for a break-in.

When she came into the brightly lit classroom in one of the university blocks, she found the man in question already installed. He was reading a paperback in a relaxed way and he looked up as she came in.

'I see you have returned,' he said, leaving Vera an opening for conversation if she wanted to take it up. A little surprised at having her arrival strategy trumped, she just raised her eyebrows and smiled rather than answer. She felt obliged to sit reasonably near him as they were the only people in the room, but she left a desk between them for decorum. He looked over at her and noted the improvement in her appearance, and then went back to his book, turning a page lightly. Vera unzipped her briefcase and took out her shot at writing a piece on an Irish heatwave, supposedly suitable for an evening paper.

'This is awful rubbish,' she said, flicking the pages over the top of the clipboard. 'I think I'll say I hadn't time to do anything.'

'Publish and be damned,' he said with a laugh, not lifting his eyes from the book. 'I mean, just read it out as if it were someone else's. Who cares anyway, besides you?'

'How do you mean?'

'They're all only interested in their own efforts. I'm sure mine is dreary in the extreme but I don't mind, one way or the other. I just want to start writing again.' He put down the paperback and looked straight at her. Vera looked straight back at him. Very attractive, she thought. Why is he bothering to talk to me? Amusing himself, I suppose, just as I am amusing myself with him. What am I thinking of? she asked herself, and then the other participants began to filter in, along with the lecturer.

The session began and everyone had to read their piece aloud. Some were reasonably good and one or two were like school compositions, including Vera's. The man beside her had taken a humorous angle and the piece was quite funny, but the wit was lost on the lecturer who began to dissect it and missed its point.

'Humour is tricky,' she warned him, when he mentioned that he had intended it to be funny. 'Avoid it for the present, it's too early to introduce it.' He took back his piece and glanced at his critic without any expression.

At the break Vera and her new acquaintance seemed to

turn to one another naturally, and to her surprise she heard herself saying:

'We might as well introduce ourselves. I'm Vera Nolan.'

'And I'm Dan Devereux. I'm from Wexford, but I've been away for years and I'm just back, picking up the threads, so to speak.'

'I used to know parts of Wexford well. We took a house for some years at Saint Helen's when the children were small. It has probably changed a lot since then.' She hadn't intended to give a potted biography of herself, but it sounded like one: married with family now grown up, likes the sea, and so on. He didn't ask her any further questions nor did she ask any. A slight nervousness had made her prattle on. They were at the class to study writing, for God's sake and not other people's lives, and anyway a ten week course would give opportunities for conversation. At the end of the second session Dan Devereux got up first.

'Goodbye until next week,' he said, smiling at her, and went out with the first of the leave-takers. Vera tidied up. She felt suddenly silly. It was years since she had made an effort to please anyone and here she was trying to be pleasant to this man, and wasn't even adept at it.

'Do you feel your writing is developing, or at least a wish to write?' the lecturer asked her as she passed by.

'No great hopes. I'm finding it a bit daunting. I'm not sure where to start on next week's piece on current affairs.'

'Try anyway, that's the important thing,' the lecturer said in a somewhat games mistressy tone. 'I want you all to recognise that successful short pieces are the lead-in to anything more ambitious you may have in mind.' Vera rolled her eyes and left.

Abdul Shamir, an arab from the United Arab Emerites visiting Dublin, opened his newspaper as he sat in a comfortable armchair in the foyer of Dublin's Dalton Hotel. Thirty-five years old, and working as an international trade journalist, he had

30

come over to Dublin for the launch of a new chemical product that one of the firms which employed his services had created. The Dalton, an elegant, friendly place at any time, is particularly welcoming in cold or sharp spring weather, and he found a comfortable seat beside the open fire. As he waited for a business contact to collect him, he read through the business advertisements in *The Irish Times*. When he had glanced through the main business advertisements, he turned to the categorised columns, and an advertisement caught his eye.

> PR practice starting up small scale. Principal interested in acquiring minority partner. Please detail transferable accounts and financial investment envisaged. Replies to Box 3888IT.

Shamir circled it in pen. A small public relations business could be of interest, because he needed a further contact in Dublin, in order to test out an idea he had had in mind for some time. If the advertiser were sound, and a cash injection made his interest viable, this might be simple enough: privacy would be paramount. He went on reading the paper and then he took out his briefcase and drew up an answer to the advertisement, and addressed it to the box number. He sauntered over to the mail box beside the entrance of the hotel and dropped in his reply just as his business contact arrived. They greeted one another and strolled out into the bright morning sunshine of St Stephen's Green, a fine park opposite the hotel.

Brian Nolan opened his *Irish Times* and turned immediately to the categorised business advertisements. Feeling isolation descending on him every morning as he started work in his study, he had taken to reading the advertisements closely, instead of scanning them, looking for motivation. Now he concentrated on them almost excessively.

> PR practice starting up small scale. Principal interested in acquiring minority partner. Please detail transferable accounts and financial investment envisaged. Replies to Box 3888IT.

Brian read the advertisement a second time, and then a third. Maybe this was the kind of thing to go for? He was finding out plenty about himself since he had retired, and one realisation was that the reason some people can stay comfortably in the one organisation for most of their working life may be that they are actually incapable of working on their own. He saw that success in one field does not necessarily mean success in another, and he had become scared that his ideas of new business rolling in to him in answer to the promotional letters for his facilities were possibly pie in the sky. Some polite enquiries had arrived following his initial direct mail shot, but nothing had developed as yet. Telephone calls he had made to former contacts had proved somewhat embarrassing and unfruitful. He booted up his computer and answered the advertisement, sealed his reply in an envelope and went out to post it.

Dan Devereux got into his dark green BMW and set off for Dublin early in the afternoon. He would spend some time in town making specific purchases, have a pleasant meal early-ish and go along to the writers' course.

Dan was forty-one, and had retired as a test pilot in the United States. He had come back to live in County Wexford, where the family home and land had come to him on the death of his father. When he was nineteen he had left Wexford, and as he had been at boarding school for his secondary education, he had no ties and few contacts there. After many years in the States and a childless marriage which had ended in separation, and eventual divorce, he found himself at the top of his profession, but very much alone as a person. He had had various woman friends, but had not found anyone with whom he could settle down; he was just beginning to believe that he wasn't the kind of person who could make and sustain a loving relationship. Then his remaining parent, his father, had died and his married sister had not contested the will which left the home and land to him, if he came back and settled there. It would have been easy enough to stay in the States and cross over to some other profession for which his years as a test pilot would fit him, but he hadn't needed the money and felt he should sort out this change in circumstances. He then came back to Ireland to review his life before breaking into something else. He had never farmed, but the land at Garrycloe was sandy and well drained and he planned to get expert advice about it.

Dan had done some writing in the States, but led too varied a life to stick at it, and now that he was back in Ireland, he thought he might try again. Joining the writing course was a means of collecting his thoughts and getting back some discipline, and attending the course in Dublin gave him the privacy and freedom he wanted. He sped along the smooth highway that runs from Rosslare port to Dublin through County Wicklow, also known as 'The Garden Of Ireland', and as he drove along he thought about Vera Nolan. He couldn't quite make out why she interested him, and he didn't even think he liked her much, but there was lots of life in her, and this was something he found attractive. She seemed to have caught the writing bug, but he didn't think she would make anything of it. Still, there seemed to be some electricity between them and he idly wondered should he ask her out to dinner some evening. Of course she had a husband and grown up children, but dinner once or twice might be interesting and he was feeling the solitariness of having everything he needed, money, privacy, freedom to go where he liked and do as he chose, and no ties. He half thought of writing a novel, and he fancied the idea of having an older woman as one of the main characters. It would be fun to study such a woman closely and get to know her. Vera Nolan would fit the role and maybe she would accept an invitation for the following week. He had a sneaking feeling that their brief meetings were having an effect on her, and smiled at the ongoing improvement in her grooming and dressing since their initial encounter. Women were easy enough to read, he thought. It was a matter of remembering

33

what had been in the pages before. There would be plenty of attractive women in and around Wexford, particularly around Festival time, when the world and his wife came for the annual international opera season, but the idea of an out-of-town dinner date amused him and he decided that he would invite Vera Nolan and see what happened.

Dorothy walked down to *The Irish Times* office during her lunch break to collect any replies to her advertisement. She moved with a swing these days, as new ideas and possibilities presented themselves, and her very positivity seemed to keep her pointed in the right direction. As a sportswoman she was particularly interested in sports tourism, feeling that Ireland could offer first class activities in this line. The number of leisure centres in resorts was increasing, and she had a positive response to preliminary enquiries about promoting their facilities professionally. She was recording the calls at home and processing them each evening, as she went ahead with other preparations, getting letter heads printed and looking around for the right accountant. She only hoped her going away present wouldn't be something ornamental and could be used in her new practice, but as she was keeping her plans a secret, it would probably end up being something fancy. She laughed at the idea of her coveting something practical. Maybe they wouldn't give her a present at all!

Over a cup of coffee in Bewleys with Kate, she opened the three replies she had picked up. The first was a six-page letter from an obvious lunatic, which she dropped into her handbag unread. The next was from Abdul Shamir, an Arab businessman staying in the Dalton Hotel, which set her back on her heels, as an immediate appointment was suggested. The reason given was the short period that Mr Shamir would be in Dublin, and this made the whole concept go into the second round of development, before she had fully thought out the first. She laid the letter carefully on the table for re-reading and consideration.

'Kate, you're not going to believe this one. It's from Brian Nolan!'

'Brian Nolan! Well, there's a quare one for you. I thought you told me he was up and flying, as far as you knew. Something must have upset his apple tart, if he is contacting a box number.'

'Brian, of all people,' murmured Dorothy, still reading his reply. 'Here he is, modestly asking for the favour of a meeting to discuss common ground.' She burst out laughing, thinking it just too funny that Brian should be seeking common ground with someone who had run his office for him for years. 'Cards-close-to-the-chest-Nolan', who had left with such an air of purpose, has answered her advertisement.

'Well, you'll have to think that one out, certainly.'

'I won't rush in. Still, good old Brian mightn't be the worst as a business contact, but no form of partnership would be on the table. Too set in his ways and too far on in life. Never one to take a risk. I need new thinking now. Oh, there's still this reply from Abdul Shamir.'

They read the note together. The letter was written on the finest quality paper and the address was in Riyadh, United Arab Emerites, with an accommodation address at the Dalton Hotel. He said he came to Europe about four times a year working with a variety of products, and that he needed a base with office facilities, so that his Irish accounts could be managed and their products promoted when necessary. He referred briefly to oil by-products, so Dorothy had no specific information on whatever it was she might be required to promote. He mentioned financial investment, saying that this would present no difficulty, and money transfers could be effected whenever necessary.

'I like the last part of his letter,' said Kate. 'I wouldn't mind seeing Arab oil money pouring into something I had up and running. All that's missing is a very handsome face, deep brown eyes, tons of charm and style, and a slice of an airline!'

'Ah stop. You're not taking this seriously, and neither am

I! It can't do me any harm to go along and have a look at him, now can it? It might be just the way to get going.'

Dorothy made up her mind to meet Mr Shamir and hear what he had to say. As her letter heads wouldn't be back from the designer for proofing for a few days, she decided to phone the Dalton and make an appointment.

'I'd go for that Arab gentleman,' said Kate. 'I'll be dying to know what's going on underneath his cloak and dagger.'

Vera finished her current affairs piece to be read out at the writers' group session that evening. She read it through and thought it very trivial. For God's sake, she couldn't be creative, even when she tried! The piece seemed devoid of interest and she felt like giving up the whole idea. Maybe she wouldn't bother turning up at all, although it wasn't her form to give up so easily, but she felt it in her bones that this course was simply going to show her up as a person who would never be able to write anything worthwhile. In spite of herself she thought of Dan Devereux, and knew that if she gave up going to the course, she would miss the weekly encounter. She'd go one more time.

To celebrate this momentous decision she got ready with great care, first having a luxuriant perfumed bath to re-establish her self-esteem, washing and colour-rinsing her hair until it shone reddish brown, and then dressing in one of her two suits which she reserved for formal occasions. A pair of good court shoes finished off the look. Usually her clothes were sporty and easy-fitting, but she knew the suit would give her style, and she softened the effect with some costume jewellery which she had bought on holidays in Israel. She finished off her hair with her battery tongs and gave it a smart swinging shape which framed her face. She told herself that this was the first and last time that she would dress up for a night class, and she felt that it would give the impression that she had a more exciting life to live, when she failed to turn up at the following sessions. So used was Vera to imagining how other

36

people perceived her that she quite overlooked the fact that the people in the class would have no particular interest in her, apart, possibly, from Dan Devereux. She said 'Good night' to Brian from the hall, on her way out, so that he wouldn't notice how well-dressed she was.

When she arrived at the class there was no Dan Devereux, and she was taken aback at her own disappointment. She settled down to listen to the lecturer in order to distract herself from her thoughts and, to her surprise, Dan did eventually appear, well after the break. He slipped in and sat in the nearest empty seat, without looking around. At the end she pretended to talk to the woman beside her, comparing notes on the difficulties of writing anything decent, and when she got up to go, she saw that Dan was waiting at the door. As she drew level with him, he said, 'See you for a minute, if that's all right?' It came more as a statement than a question, and Vera found herself nodding in assent. As they left the room they fell into step along the glassed-in corridor leading down to the exit doors.

'I'd like to invite you to dinner some time soon,' Dan said pleasantly. 'Is there any hope that my invitation might be accepted?'

'Well, I hardly think so. And, for various reasons, I may not be going on with the course.' She looked at him with a superior smile and left it to him to continue.

'What about coming for a drink right now? If you agree to come, I'll tell you what delayed me, and if we run out of conversation you'll have to think of something to fill in the time. Some adventure or other.' Vera was immediately stimulated by the confidence of his manner in inviting her and she thought for a moment. It would be a pity to waste the effort she had put into getting ready for this evening, and her smart suit and high heels made her feel sexy and attractive.

'Oh, all right. We could drop over to the Clifford Hotel, across from the college.' She was proud of her cool manner of accepting.

'That would be really nice,' said Dan, quite surprised at her ready acceptance. He had thought she would play around with the idea, and probably back out of it. 'I'm sure we will find plenty to talk about over a drink, so I'll tell you now why I was so late this evening.' At this stage they were walking down to the car park to collect their respective cars. 'I hit a fox crossing the road and it was thrown up on the bonnet of the car. I couldn't see ahead for a few moments, and travelling at a fair speed it was something of an impact.'

'Don't tell me you travelled to Dublin with a fox on the front of the car. Where is it?' Vera enquired.

'No. Of course not. When I got back control of the car I ran into the car in front, so that took some sorting out. Luckily the carcass of the poor animal was caught in the front bumper so I had evidence of what had happened. Still no one but the fox was hurt and the insurance company will settle it in due course. Now is that a proper excuse for a late arrival?'

Vera was amused at his way of telling the story, as if he had made it up to entertain her.

'I don't remember asking for an explanation,' she said archly and laughed out loud. Then she got into her car to drive across to the hotel, waved lightly, and asked herself what she was doing meeting this man for a drink.

3

VERA DROVE across to the hotel and luckily found a parking place at the entrance. She took off her coat, which would have hidden her suit, rolled it up and put it in the boot, moving quickly so that she would be inside before Dan arrived. She went into the foyer and down to the powder room, where she ran a comb through her hair. She rather liked her reflection in the mirror and, with a sense of occasion, she added another touch of lipstick. She always used a good one, if she bothered at all. When she emerged, Dan Devereux was waiting in the foyer, and he smiled appreciatively at her as she came towards him, and, looking back much later, she was to remember that it was as she crossed the reception area to join him that she fell in love for the very first time in her life.

Vera Nolan, fifty-three years of age, who had spent all her life calculating and controlling, taking and measuring, and conditioning others to expect less from her than she expected from them, had just fallen in love. Brian and she had never been in love. They had such similar views on living skills, and had therefore got on so well together, that they had not annoyed each other about their expectations. Instead they had gone into marriage with their eyes wide open, and instinctively worked out a sufficiently happy and balanced lifestyle to please both of them. They had done it much as business partners might arrive at a good relationship, with a profitable outcome for their enterprise as their binding force. There had been some first class shouting matches down the years, and sometimes Vera felt she had wasted herself on a very dull man, but she always ended by realising that Brian actually suited her quite well.

Now, looking at Dan Devereux waiting for her across the wide, brightly lit foyer, she knew he was making her want him in half a dozen ways at once, and her mixed feelings were spiced with the excitement of the unknown. She had suggested this hotel for its convenience and busy atmosphere, with its notice boards signalling various meetings of residents' associations, companies and private dinner parties. Groups of people moved here and there and the feeling was pleasant and sociable. She could have been attending any of the meetings, and this gave her a feeling of freedom. It was exactly the right place to come for that casual drink.

They walked through the crowded, warm and dimly lit lounge together, and found a table at the very back in the porch-type annexe.

'Gin and tonic all right, or is there something more exciting, you'd fancy?'

'Gin and tonic is just fine. I always think attending a night class needs rewarding, although I imagine that this is the last reward that I'll be around for. I just know that I'll never write anything anyone will want to read, apart from my will, that is, and that's already written.'

'Don't be so morbid. Of course you may write, and even if you don't, you'll probably do something more interesting. There are too many aspiring writers for all of them to get published, one way or the other. It's a sort of craze these days and publishers must be really sick of typescripts arriving through their letter boxes from hopefuls, young or otherwise.'

'Not so much of the "otherwise",' said Vera and laughed as she said it, feeling ridiculously at ease, a little lit up and loosened. Normally she would have been busy manipulating the conversation, but now she was just floating along, not caring who said what. It was a strange liquid feeling and she was revelling in it.

'Now to business,' said Dan. 'We'll talk about writing again. You are looking really lovely this evening, and I want to know will you come and have dinner with me some time soon? Come on, say you will.'

'As a married woman I can't just go off to dinner like that, with a man I don't know.'

'Of course you can. That's the best way to get to know him.'

'And what's so important about getting to know him?' asked Vera, staring him out.

'Same again,' said Dan to the passing bar attendant. 'Now, where were we? Oh yes, you can't find that out in advance. Catch twenty-two situation. Well, will you come?'

'I don't think so. At least I'll have to think about it. Married women don't accept dinner invitations that easily in my culture. And how about you – is there a Mrs Dan?'

'No Missus Dan. Long ago there was a short, explosive marriage and an American divorce. Tracey was a Protestant, and I was a Catholic and I didn't have any difficulty getting the divorce through in the States. No details now, if you don't mind. I asked you over here so that we could enjoy a chat, not to roll back the carpet of life and gaze at the floorboards.'

He looked at her steadily and said, firmly and slowly: 'And how easily do married woman accept dinner invitations in your culture? I mean, do I have to ask three times or something of that ilk?'

'Don't be silly, you know what I mean.'

'Tell me, Vera, are you happy this evening? I mean are you feeling happy right now?'

'What a funny question. It's pleasant enough here, and in fact, now that I think of it, I'll have to be going soon.'

'You will, but you have to deal with the other half of that gin and tonic before you do. It'll be along in a minute. I just want to say that you look dynamite, sitting there in your beautifully tailored suit. That shade of brown suits you, by the way. I love your thick shiny hair and the slightly haughty glances you throw out from side to side. You're a veritable power house of a person, my dear Vera.'

'I'm not your dear Vera, so less of that,' said Vera, but not crossly as she was enjoying herself so much. He changed his tone to a more casual one.

'What do you think of the recent weather? There's a great stretch in the evenings, now isn't there? I'm sure it's grand weather for sowing. Have you your crops down yet?'

Vera had to giggle. Dan took the drinks from the waiter's tray and by mutual consent they sat back to enjoy them. They laughed and chatted through the second drink and then it was Dan who suggested smoothly that they should go. He saw her attentively to her car.

'Vera, dinner? Yes or no?' Vera stood under the spot-lit palm trees in the hotel car park, and heard the leaf blades rustling and said nothing.

'Vera, I'm asking you to dinner. Do I have to ask you three times in your, ahem, culture? Will you or will you not come out to dinner with me, say next week?'

As he said it she could feel that he was absolutely serious, although he was using jocose words.

'Is it yes or no?'

'It's yes, Dan.'

'Wonderful!' His eyes lit up with pleasure. Vera knew unequivocally that she had given her consent to something which she couldn't measure, for it is the first concession that counts. After that it is only a matter of detail, timing, and location for the unrolling of a relationship.

Brian Nolan waited for two weeks for something to happen, once he had answered the advertisement about the new PR agency starting up. He was enveloped in depression, and forlornly hoped against hope that he would be contacted by someone with a proposition for him. Then he realised he should cut his losses and learn from life, by copying the idea and inserting a similar one himself. He would put in something about opening an agency, without specifying what he intended to offer, just saying he was interested in a professional partner and possible investor.

He had a definite project in mind, a pet project for himself and people like him, who were forced to retire while they were still fully fit, and wanted desperately to continue in the work force, people who wanted to be out there in the mainstream, when society told them they were past it. He had read about 'Grey Power' in the States and the idea fascinated him. Many older people in good health had money, frustrated ambition, and a dread of being closed in with nothing to do beyond hobbies, and, frequently, not sufficient spiritual values to keep them feeling balanced. Brian saw an opening for a commercially viable agency, which would cater for their needs. Maybe there were people out there who wanted to do exciting things, just once or twice, but wanted to do them all the same. An agency could put them in touch with the right people, for a percentage of the fee involved. He was obsessed with the idea of breaking out of this web, but he lacked the inherent drive required to get a business off the ground by himself. Maybe his advertisement would bring in the person with the ingredient he was missing. He couldn't bear to discuss the idea with anyone, even Vera, who might have laughed at it, and he had always had such a fear of ridicule, that his nick-name 'Cards-close-to-the-chest-Nolan' had been well-earned.

'Service starting on agency basis, small scale, with view to development. Mature people with specific skills should apply. Replies to Box No ...' was the final draft of his advertisement. He phoned the newspaper, found out the cost, and posted it along with a cheque. *Nihil desperandum,* he told himself mournfully, trying to drag himself out of his depression.

Dorothy Reynolds picked up the paper in her office and surveyed the business page. She turned to the small advertisements and concentrated as she read:

Service starting on agency basis, small scale, with view to development. Mature people with specific skills should apply. Replies to Box No. 4010 IT.

Wonder what they are going to flog, she thought. Maybe they

43

want a service promoted. It would be nice to have a second string, besides the leisure facilities promotion she had in mind. There might be something there for Dorothy, she mused and put a reply in the post that day.

Abdul Shamir waited in the foyer of the Dalton Hotel to meet Dorothy Reynolds. She had agreed to an appointment with him, and he hoped it would go well. He also hoped that she would not be a very young woman, but would be attractive nonetheless, as business would go better with maturity to draw on. He intended to import cosmetic products into Ireland, and to investigate Irish-made cosmetics for possible export, and a business address in Dublin, the use of a small office and a fair measure of privacy were vital to him.

Dorothy dressed for the appointment. She had taken a sum of money out of her account and gone to one of the leading boutiques. 'Dress me. I'm starting my own business,' she had said to the saleswoman. The effect had been excellent. The navy suit and first rate accessories gave her an air of style and authority and the six-weeks dieting had paid off. A new hair style gave her face a fresh image. As she came through the entrance door, Shamir liked what he saw, and hoped this was the woman he was meeting. Dorothy reached the appointed part of the foyer and he approached her with a charming smile.

'Abdul Shamir,' he said, stretching out his hand. 'You must be Ms Dorothy Reynolds. I'm delighted to meet you.' Dorothy met his smile.

'Dorothy Reynolds. How do you do?' They moved into the lounge together and found a table by the window. Abdul Shamir signalled, and immediately a waiter was by the table. Attractive and authoritative, thought Dorothy. I wonder what he wants from Dublin. Shamir waited until afternoon tea had arrived, and asked the waiter to serve it, before turning the full battery of his personality on his new business contact.

The offer he made was interesting. When they had discussed his ideas thoroughly, he said that if her agency would handle his account, he would be in a position to make a substantial payment in advance. He would expect his products to be well promoted, and she would be handling something quite new in cosmetics on the European market. He would need storage space, not much, but sufficient to keep a small flow of supply, and he would pay her well for her services. She would not see him often. It sounded a very good offer, but Dorothy did not agree immediately, although she was anxious to have at least two good accounts before giving up her job, feeling that it was better not to jump at the first offer. She listened carefully to Abdul Shamir's proposals, and asked him to expect to hear from her, care of his accommodation address at the hotel. Eventually they bid one another a friendly though formal goodbye, and as Dorothy walked away from the hotel, she decided that Shamir would indeed be her first customer.

Frank Donegan snapped the top back on a large tube of Flake White oil paint and wiped his hands on a cloth. God, how he loved painting! To do what you want in life, and to be paid for it must be one of the most exciting forms of life imaginable. Today Frank thought he was winning all the way. The painting had gone well for him; his large commission from a Canadian academic was coming on nicely and the fee for it would allow him to paint whatever he liked for the remainder of the year. Sometimes, when he was least expecting it, the work flourished, and he would quite likely have the commission finished for his exhibition in three months' time. An exhibition needed a high point in the form of an outstanding work and this could well be it. He made himself a cup of espresso coffee and sat at his studio window to think about Dorothy Reynolds.

It was strange that Dorothy should have come back into his mind after all these years. She must have only been eighteen when he had first seen her, leaping with life when they met on holidays on Achill Island. He was only a few years older than she was, and within twenty-four hours they had fallen madly, crazily in love. Within a week he knew the feel of her smooth wind- and sun-tanned skin, as he held her to him beneath the old-fashioned coarse white sheets of the Achill guest house under the shadows of Dooagh mountain. How they had laughed and loved in that old annexe behind the guest house, where the *bean a tigh* had put him in a wooden extension building which smelled of damson jam, warm and sweet under the western sun. Getting Dorothy to and from the annexe had been a matter of leaving back doors open for easy passage, with plenty of whispering and giggling, and when she had returned to her job in Dublin, he had stayed on to paint the changing light over Keem Bay, the multi-coloured islands in the Atlantic ocean and the dramatic cliffs at the other end of Achill. He had missed her sorely, but had rejoiced at the thought of their reunion in Dublin, and he had painted his heart out during the few weeks that he had stayed on, not minding too much when he had not heard from her. As she put it, 'I'm a rotten correspondent, but I'll be jumping out of my skin to see you again. Honestly, I wouldn't know what to say to you on a telephone, I'm so in love with you!' Frank had taken to throwing himself into the Atlantic waves off Keem Bay when his desire to make love to her became too much for him.

When he returned to Dublin six weeks later, there was no sign of Dorothy. She was nowhere to be found and he was aghast. He searched the town to no avail, finding out that she had taken severance from her job and given a month's notice to the landlord of her Lower Baggot Street apartment. Her disappearance was totally out of character, but then he had only known her for a few weeks' duration.

Frank was broken-hearted and bewildered. As a penniless painter he hadn't had any immediate plans for marrying Dorothy, but he knew she was very much in love with him, which would mean that all that would work itself out in time.

She had been so positive and so joyous, that he could not understand it. Dorothy had inexplicably vanished.

Frank Donegan's life changed. He emigrated to Canada to an artists' colony, where he became a fine painter in time, without losing the original wildness of his style. He painted very large pictures, as the bigger they were, the more he could express himself, and they sold well in Canada. After some years he met an American woman called Hermione, also an artist, and they teamed up, buying a large dormobile and moving as painters from area to area.

Storage of paintings had always been something of a problem, and at one stage Frank had paintings from one end of Canada to the other, stacked in art colleges, friends' basements and just about anywhere he could accommodate them. Hermione had painted flowers and plants most of the time, gathering them wherever they stopped, and her paintings were quite small, with clever, delicate detail, and fine colour combinations, displaying a tantalising freshness. They had an enjoyable and close relationship, letting one another live freely for their art, but not wanting to commit themselves in marriage, and eventually, they had decided to go their separate ways, for Hermione was ready to settle down and live in one place as an artist, without the disruption of moving around, while Frank was still a roving spirit. He felt that there simply was not enough living time for any human being, and he wanted to see all that the world had to offer, so they had parted, one sunny morning, deliberately getting up very early to face a new day without one another. As Frank had driven away, they had blessed one another for a parting without the human weakness of recrimination.

Frank had then leased a very large truck and driven all over Canada, collecting the paintings he had stored. Some of them had been damaged by damp, others had been knocked about in storage, but of the ones he liked and considered good, there was nothing that could not be repaired and renewed. He had then returned to the artists' colony where he

47

had lived originally, and held a large-scale exhibition, selling well and divesting himself of this period of his life in a satisfying way. He had kept only one painting, a painting of a west of Ireland beach, with the figure of a young, dark-haired girl running along the foam breaking on the strand, in that clarity of air peculiar to Achill, County Mayo, and he had brought this back with him when he returned to Dublin. At first he had regarded Dublin as a temporary move, thinking that he might paint in Africa for a few years, but to his surprise, he found he was ready to settle down in Ireland.

Frank was forty. He couldn't believe it himself. Forty! How could he possibly be forty! The calendar said he was, and of course he had changed a little in appearance, but he found it harder to accept ageing in himself than in others. He now wanted a relationship with a woman which would endure, someone with whom he could develop a love affair into a marriage, but it might be hard to find that someone. He decided to start the day with a stroll down Grafton Street, to see what was happening in Ireland after all these years. That was Dublin's charm. You could be away as long as you liked from it, but once back it put an arm around your shoulder and asked you how you were.

Vera Nolan went upstairs to get ready to go out to dinner with Dan Devereux. She had told Brian that she wanted to attend an extra meeting of the writers' group in a relaxed atmosphere, so it would be organised in a pub restaurant in Temple Bar, the restored artists' quarter of Dublin, down by the river Liffey. It was amazing how easily she could shut Brian out of her mind as a person, after all those years together, but it was as if she had forgotten him, and had to remind herself that he was still in her life. Brian had been so good with the children, always there, ready to row in, not demanding much, and obviously admiring her competence in running a tight ship all those years. She was positively rubbing him out, so taken over was she by her newly-aroused feelings for Dan

Devereux. Vera was in love and she was enjoying its careless rapture. This feeling was hers to savour, not to be invaded by anyone, only to be shared with Dan. She was actually jealous of herself, and fearful that she might have to share her secret somehow, when she had only just found it for herself. She had seen wives going through the hoops of cultivating a friendship, or at least an acquaintance between an exciting, newly discovered man and their husband, through contrived dinner parties or other means, but Vera wasn't going to introduce Dan Devereux to anyone, male or female. He was hers, to explore alone.

Vera worked out an outfit which would flatter her without making her look too dressed up: a white cotton loose knit, teamed with dark green leggings, as she thought this made her look 'arty'. She had bought the leggings to go with a dull tartan kilt, and now realised that the new Vera could do better. She again dried her hair in a swinging bell shape, and she approved greatly of her make-over. Sheer excitement was making her look really attractive this evening. She slipped a pair of large dark green glass earrings into her pocket which she had bought on the way home, as Brian might find her that bit too well presented for a working meeting. Then she put on a long camel coat to hide the leggings and took her clip board and note pad with her.

'Will you be late, dear?' Brian looked up as she put her head around the door to say she was off.

'I don't know, I'll go with the flow. It's part of the course to let the ideas out, and not to put a time limit on the evening. Don't wait up for me, because the chat may run on.'

Brian looked at her thoughtfully.

'Don't get carried away, now. Don't get writeritis.'

Vera raised her eyebrows and replied: 'Oh for goodness sake, don't squash my enthusiasm. It's creative writing after all, and I'll only have you to blame if I don't produce anything imaginative. I'm off now. See you.'

49

She felt a slight pang of guilt, and in order to get rid of it she swung the blame back on Brian for being dull. Vera had always put the defence of her self image before anything else. Ducking a squall of rain, she closed the hall door and got into her car quickly, first putting on the new earrings and checking their effect in the driving mirror. She put the car in gear and drove off, feeling like a young girl off on a date. Within fifteen minutes she was parking in Temple Bar where Dan had arranged to meet her.

Dan had deliberately picked a restaurant there since the risk of Vera meeting any of her acquaintances would be reduced, and he wanted her to be really relaxed that evening. A smaller, more intimate place would tell its own tale were she to run into anyone who would recognise her. He waited at a table with a good view of the door, in a corner of the pleasant, lively restaurant. Dan Devereux was used to succeeding in making people like him, particularly women, and he wanted Vera not only to like him, but to fall in love with him. He thought there might be a river of passion hidden in just such a woman, and he was excited about the possibility of finding out if this were so. He fancied the idea of enjoying the experience and, hopefully, leading her to enjoy it too – and therein might lie a good story for a play or novel.

Vera crossed the restaurant to where he was sitting and he was struck be the way she looked. She was like someone with a very nice secret, and she had shed ten years.

'Vera, it's so good to see you. My God, how attractive you look tonight! Is this what writing has done to you, or have you some other interest that's putting a sparkle in your eye?'

'Hello Dan, are you talking nonsense already?' Vera said, flashing him a wide smile, as she had spent a long time whitening her good straight teeth and didn't want the effect to be lost on him. 'Don't forget I'm at a writers' meeting, so I'm not to be confused with compliments. I shouldn't be here at all, and well you know it!'

'I do, I do,' he said quickly, standing up and helping her

get seated.' Now that you *are* here, let's enjoy every minute of it. Come on, bring me up to date since Tuesday. Three whole days have elapsed and plenty of things must have happened. Come on, you can tell your Uncle Dan.'

4

VERA RELAXED completely as she began to sip a glass of good red wine, which Dan poured for her. It was a sensation so foreign to her that she just smiled happily across at him as she experienced it. Then a thrill of adventure ran through her. Here she was scanning a menu – but it wasn't the choice of food which excited her. It was the choice being offered to her so unexpectedly by life. In her heart she knew she had already decided what she wanted from Dan in coming out alone to dinner with him, a stranger who had moved himself skilfully into the centre of her thoughts. It might take time to work through the course of the adventure, and hopefully it would. She could not think any further than that.

Dan wanted his friendship with Vera to ripen into a liaison. He felt that a full-blown affair was his for the asking, and with a very strong character such as Vera's, the best way to handle matters was to 'go for broke' and insist on her consent. If he let things rock along, it could well turn out that Vera would come to her senses and consider it better not to see him again. Attracted to him though she might be, the habits of a lifetime are not so easily broken and the spark would, of course, burn out, and probably quite quickly. He would have to ask her before they left the restaurant.

When they were coming to the end of their leisurely meal, they sat back to sip a liqueur and prolong the evening. Then Dan leaned across the table and took her hand in such a way that she could not free it.

'Look at me, Vera,' he said, 'as I am looking at you. You must know that I want to make love to you. Will you give yourself to me, as I want to give myself to you, totally, unconditionally, for as long as you think you want the relationship? You will, won't you?'

Vera looked at him in shock. She had thought that any

talk like this would be some way down the road, and although she very much wanted to have an affair with this fascinating man, his approach was so sudden that she was genuinely knocked off balance.

'Dan, do you know what you're asking me? Of course you don't, you're a man. You couldn't know what it is for a, em ... hopefully, mature married woman to go into a love affair as suddenly as this.'

'I'm ready now, and I sense that you are. Vera, I know you'd have to manage your home and your professional life to allow for an affair, but a chance like this won't come our way again.'

'Why me, Dan? You'll meet plenty of other women.'

'Of course we'll both meet plenty of other people, and possibly be attracted to them, but this pull can't be duplicated. You feel it now, don't you? Of course you do. There's no point in my denying it, because it's dragging me across the table as I'm talking to you.'

'Dan, for God's sake let go of my hand. Honestly, you're hurting me. What's got into you? Let's talk this out.'

He released her hand, but gazed at her, without changing his expression of concentration..

'Talk away, Vera, I won't be listening. I just want to know, will you make love with me?'

'Dan, it's a crazy suggestion.'

'Listen, Vera. I've a fairly decent home near Garrycloe outside Wexford, where there's great privacy. I've no close neighbours and there's a wonderful beach for long walks, a few yards away from the house. You'd love it, and it's only two hours' drive from Dublin, at the most. We could do our love-making there.'

'I couldn't go away from home just like that,' said Vera, faltering.

'That means you want to! Of course you could. You could invent writers' conferences, or something similar. You're an intelligent woman and you don't need my feeble help to

53

organise you. Vera, don't let this marvellous opportunity slip through our hands.' He added, laughing, in a French accent: 'Listen, my leuv, com to me and I will make you the 'appiest woman in the world.'

'Dan, what a way to go on. You're making my head spin,' said Vera, so passionately that she surprised herself. A little voice in her head was saying *A married woman is expected to go through with things. Flirting is not her game. It's all or nothing.* How often she had heard phrases like that when she and women friends had been gossiping, and discussing affairs, and she had never thought, for an instant, that she would find herself at the point of agreement. But then, she *had* accepted the invitation to dinner, and done so against her better judgment. Where did she think such an invitation was leading, she asked herself now.

Dan took a different tack.

'Look Vera, I'm not going to plead with you as if you were a young girl with no life skills. I'm asking you to agree to have an affair with me, and I won't ask you again, I just couldn't.' Vera sat there, torn in two. 'Either you feel something special and powerful for me, as I do for you, and we go through this together, savouring every moment of it, or we don't see one another again.'

'Don't be silly, Dan, of course we'll meet again.'

'I'm not being silly. I'm not finishing this writing course, and I only came along the last time so that I could invite you to dinner.'

'My word, but you're a conceited man, Dan Devereux. You were quite sure I would accept, is that it?'

'Not at all. I wanted to see you again, and to go on seeing you, again and again. That was the only way to do it.'

'Look, Dan, I *do* feel you are special to me, and I've enjoyed tonight really so much, much more than I could have imagined. Can we not keep the friendship as it is, at least for a while? We'll meet again, sooner or later. You know what Ireland's like. Everyone off in all directions, mad about enjoying themselves. We'll meet by chance, if not by appointment.'

'Yes, Vera, we could meet in company, say at the Wexford Festival, or the Point Theatre, or some place like that. I don't intend to run out of Ireland at present, but if you say "no" to our taking this fantastic chance, then I'll pretend not to see you if we do meet. I'll get bad sight when you come into view, and if we are ever introduced, I'll say I've never met you before. I just couldn't go through the mechanics of polite conversation on the "How are *you*?" and 'How are *you*?' basis. There isn't enough living time left for that kind of rubbish. I can just imagine you going – "*Oh helleu, doing any writing*?" I wouldn't be bothered with that kind of thing.'

Vera was still at a loss. She was being rushed out of her control, and yet, she was deeply scared of losing this exciting man, the first man with whom she desperately wanted to have an affair. Since she had met him, her whole being seemed to be opening up, and life seemed to be offering itself in a new way. Brian crossed her mind briefly and she thought – No. Not now, this is no time to think of Brian.

'Tell me this evening that we'll make love very soon, Vera. When I think of how much I want to take you in my arms and literally rush you off your feet, the alternative is unbearable. Say you will, say you will.'

They sat there in the dim, warm restaurant, the ends of their drinks in their cupped hands and the gulf of Vera's hesitation between them. The time ticked slowly by and although the background noise was sympathetic and constant, the silence between them was interminable. At last Vera could bear it no longer. She lifted her eyes, and gazed into his, which were unflinching, waiting for her answer.

'Yes, Dan, I will.'

Frank Donegan bought a copy of *The Irish Times* and went into Bewleys to have coffee and read it. He settled himself into a corner and read the front page and the editorial, and then turned to the small business advertisements. A collection of paintings he had done in Canada had turned up in a storage unit, just when he had thought they were untraceable, and he had also been painting busily since his return to Dublin. He might find someone through the advertisements who would be suitable to run an exhibition for him, and take care of the public relations and publicity side of the enterprise. That way he could hand over all the troublesome part of it and concentrate on painting. He planned to mount an exhibition in two months' time and was looking around for a venue. The booking of the venue, the printing of the invitations, press coverage, catalogue compilation and staffing for its duration would have to be done professionally, and of course he could get a gallery to do it all for him. He hadn't any business connections in Dublin, nor did he want to impose on the few social contacts he had made through having a drink here and there. His eye fell on an advertisement saying:

> PR service starting up small scale. Principal interested in acquiring minority partner. Please detail transferable accounts and financial investment envisaged. Replies to Box 3888IT.

It interested him. He wouldn't be interested in any type of partnership, but maybe he could discuss the launch of his exhibition with these people and, if they were suitable, let them take him and his painting over. A small public relations business could prove to be a good commercial contact. It might be worth a throw. He drafted a reply on the back of an envelope and slipped it into his pocket. When he had finished his coffee and newspaper, he walked out into the fresh Dublin morning and strolled down to the newspaper office, to drop his reply into their box. Life seemed to be taking on an interesting aspect. Good old Dublin, never lets you down, he thought.

A few days later, Brian arranged to have any replies to his advertisement posted on to him. When he opened the only reply envelope and Dorothy's answer fell out, he leaned back at his desk and laughed. So, Dorothy was also setting up on her own. There they had been, two people working closely in an organisation, both intending to go into private practice, and neither had trusted the other sufficiently to even mention, much less discuss their plans. Maybe they could join forces after all. Then he thought of his reply to the somewhat similar advertisement which had prompted him to take action. Of course it must have been Dorothy's advertisement. And there had been no reply from her to date. What a laugh *she* must have had at him, arrogant, secretive Brian Nolan, who had cleaned out the shelf of reference books in his former office without as much as leaving a list behind him of what he had taken, answering a small advertisement, in order to ride on someone else's initiative. And then she had answered *his* advertisement! She was obviously only trawling for business, while he was looking for a life-buoy.

Suddenly it did not seem so funny after all. Dorothy Reynolds, the person he had tried to keep back with faint praise and no recommendations in the right places, with his overweening determination that she would only work for *him*, was now the person throwing him a life-buoy. He suddenly felt mortally ashamed, ashamed of the small-mindedness which had eroded him. The feeling swept unexpectedly over him, in recurring waves, and there was no escaping it. It was like floodgates of embarrassment opening at the realisation that he was a very small person indeed, with stunted self-development. Brian Nolan was overcome by sadness and he leaned across his desk, took off his glasses and wept on to the backs of his hands for the first time since he was a child. He was greatly relieved that he was alone in the house, for Vera could never have understood this turn in his thinking, and could not have helped him, much less coped with him. After a minute or two he pulled out his handkerchief and mopped his face, knowing that he had hit rock-bottom, and that upwards was the only way that he could go now. Real sorrow can sometimes be a gift in disguise, and *il y a une certaine sat-*

isfaction à se sentir profondément triste.

In his newly-found humility Brian decided to screw up his courage and phone Dorothy at the agency. Maybe she hadn't left yet. He would surely have been asked back to her farewell party, having left so recently, himself. She must be still there. Before his resolution weakened, he reached for the telephone and dialled her direct line. She came on straight away, and he didn't know whether to put down the phone immediately, or to be grateful to hear her voice. He plunged in.

'Dorothy, hello, Brian Nolan here. How are things? Are you surprised to hear from me?'

Brian had always resorted to asking questions whenever he was embarrassed, and here he was, at it again.

'Brian, hello! Good to hear from you,' said Dorothy in a surprised voice.

'I'll go straight in on this one, Dorothy, that is, if you have a minute to listen to me.'

'Of course I have a minute. Brian, what *is* it?'

Brian rushed at it.

'First I must say that was my advertisement that you answered! Just as I answered yours! I mean the ones in *The Irish Times*. You probably wouldn't be in the slightest interested, but Dorothy, I would greatly appreciate meeting you again, if you had even the vaguest interest in doing a project with me. You see, um, I've something in mind.'

'That's a great speech,' said Dorothy in her breezy way. What she was thinking was 'Imagine old Brian grovelling'. She wanted to shriek with laughter.

'Brian, this is a killer,' she said. 'Yes, I *am* going out on my own. I haven't told the folks here in the agency, so keep it under your hat until I do. I wouldn't be able for all the question and answer sessions from people who would never do anything like that.'

'Of course I will. I didn't say much about plans at my own departure.'

'I must say it never crossed my mind that I was answering your advertisement. *Of course* I'll meet you. We'll have a good laugh over it, if nothing else. How has life been with you, anyway?'

'I can't say it's been great, Dorothy. I know there's plenty to be done out there, but I don't seem to be able to get down to it. May I take you to lunch, some day soon?'

'I'd be delighted, Brian. Let's make a date now. I could make Thursday or Friday, and how about you?'

'I hate to say it, but I could make it any day. Thursday sounds great. I'll book somewhere. Can I phone you on Wednesday, just to arrange the venue and meeting time?'

'I'm looking forward to it already.'

'Dorothy, thank you so much. I think you've saved my life!'

'I'll be most interested as to how, Brian, but that'll keep until Thursday. Cheers for now.'

Brian pulled out his files for 'Beyond the Grey' with new enthusiasm, and pored over them. He set about making a data base and listing possible interests for older people, the services available to them, and the gaps in those services. He had scoured American and British magazines, picking up hints on selective interest travel, articles on returning to previous interests, new and unusual skills to acquire, social services and health and fitness tips. He had also been studying financial arrangements and offers for the older person, short-term investment plans, and high-interest schemes. He was a methodical worker and he was enjoying what he was doing.

'Brian, the room is quite dark. Did you not put on a light or two?' It was Vera returning from work.

'I got dug into something,' Brian answered. 'Some day soon I hope I can tell you about it, but I'm only thinking it out at this stage. Have you anything in mind for dinner? I'm suddenly quite hungry, and I didn't notice it until now.'

'Ask me first how did my day go, then I'll do something

about dinner.' Vera was feeling not a little guilty about her night out with Dan and the decision she had made about him. She felt she should chat for a few moments before going into the kitchen as usual.

'Sorry, Vera, how did it go? Any problems?'

'Not really. Career counselling is career counselling, and the same questions come up again and again. I can't live their young lives for them, but I can point them in the direction I think might suit them. There isn't a great deal of satisfaction in it.'

Brian nodded, thinking privately, as he had done for years, that maybe the young people weren't getting sufficient satisfaction out of her counselling either. Vera went out to the kitchen and he got up and poured two glasses of good dry sherry, bringing hers out to the kitchen. He was actually celebrating his new feeling of reality.

A month later, the noise at Dorothy Reynolds' going away party waxed and waned, and Dorothy, the centre of attraction, laughed off the compliments which were being freely given. She was wearing one of her new suits and she was feeling great, and as she moved about, she was the envy of everyone for having the courage to go out on her own. Admittedly she still had a mortgage to pay off, but her colleagues saw that as an incentive to do very well.

Dorothy handled the applause graciously and warmly, and the evening got off to a flying start. She circulated among friends and colleagues, and made light of her new venture.

'Dorothy, you look so chic. Leaving us has turned you into a Parisienne.'

'Oh, come on now, you're buttering me up.'

'I suppose wedding bells will be the next sound from your direction.'

'Nonsense, I'll have my new business to get going, not a marriage!'

She moved off, laughing, leaving the two men reflecting

about her.

'Some people are complete in themselves, and she is one of them. She's like an egg. Shell, white and yolk. The lot. She doesn't need anyone, really.'

'That kind of woman could break a man's heart, if he were foolish enough to love her.'

It was a great evening, and Dorothy enjoyed it to the full, but all the same, she wanted to go home alone in a taxi. She had been out for meals several times with friends and colleagues at the agency over the past few weeks, and had been invited to lunch with the board of directors, and now she wanted to walk alone into her own home, which from tonight would be her new business premises. When the right moment came, she was grabbed and kissed by everyone and she left the party as it was winding down.

Dorothy slipped into a house coat and stretched out on her couch and relaxed, switching on the television. Just as she went to choose a channel the telephone rang.

'Good evening. This is Abdul Shamir calling from the Dalton Hotel. May I speak to Ms Dorothy Reynolds please?'

'This is Dorothy Reynolds, Mr Shamir, but aren't you calling a little late in the evening?'

'Please excuse me for doing so,' said Shamir. 'I have only arrived back into Dublin and I am leaving for London at lunch time tomorrow. When we met recently I did not consider contacting you at such an unsuitable time, but now I am wondering if you could possibly make yourself free at such short notice, and meet me tomorrow morning?' His approach was apologetic but assertive. She thought for a moment, and realised that her life had taken a new direction, and she had better go with it.

'Very well, Mr Shamir. Can you telephone me again at nine o'clock in the morning and I will see what can be done?'

'Certainly. I look forward to it. Good night, Ms Reynolds and thank you very much for taking my call.'

Dorothy said goodbye and lay back on her couch. This man seemed very interested indeed to do business with her. Tomorrow would be her first day in her own PR practice and she had decided that he would be her first client.

She rose early next morning, showered and dressed with care in a well cut street dress. When Shamir phoned her at exactly nine o'clock, they arranged to meet at the Dalton Hotel. If that meeting went well they could do business from her office at home.

Her home was regularly cleaned to sparkling level by a firm of professional cleaners. The dining-room was now a sunny office with fax and filing cabinets installed, and it looked business-like and pleasant. The small ante-room which had been her breakfast room would be suitable for a full-time secretary, and her drawing-room would be her reception area.

Dorothy joined Abdul Shamir for a morning coffee and they talked through his plans for the launch of a cosmetic product derived from eastern oils. It was a coincidence that she had so recently been working with cosmetics, and this pleased Mr Shamir. They then went by taxi to see her premises and discuss the matter further. Shamir's manners were impeccable, his bank references faultless, his grasp of the Irish market quite up to the minute, and his business manner very pleasing. He looked over Dorothy's premises politely and said they were perfect for the handling of his business. Then he asked her if she wanted an advance in fees for her services. Dorothy decided to run with her luck and agreed.

'That will enable me to go straight ahead with your work, rather than put it aside while I attend to something that would give a financial yield more gradually.'

'That is what I have in mind. And now may I use your telephone?'

He spoke briefly, first in Arabic and then in English, and then, with everything in place, he smiled his lovely slow Eastern smile, and said he must go. Dorothy let him out and once again, within twenty-four hours, relaxed on her couch and smiled at life. There was so much of interest going on already.

Vera sat into her armchair in the study after dinner, where Brian was relaxing with the end of his glass of wine. The sound of the television was turned down and he was flicking through a periodical. She thought this might be a good time to broach the matter of going away for a weekend on her own at short notice, and decided to present it as a 'writers' weekend'. When she had given her 'yes' to Dan, she had given it because she knew he meant what he said, and that he would not ask her a second time. The sheer amorality of the proposal had shocked and thrilled her. All her life Vera had followed Christian values and still did, but this blast of pressure from her outside life was something she could not turn down. Middle-aged women are not fools, and Vera had the sexual curiosity of the good-living. She was also quite besotted with this attractive stranger who had challenged her to widen her horizons, sexually and otherwise. The fact that she was being wildly unfaithful to Brian now seemed irrelevant, when it came to her feelings for Dan Devereux, for one man seemed to blot out the other like the moon slipping behind a dark cloud, a *Mondfinsternis* or unexpected darkening of the moon. She was so grateful that the two boys were in residence at College, because their presence would have embarrassed her desperately, and would then have quickly brought her to her senses. They would certainly have noticed her acting out of character, and possibly confused her into giving it up. As it was, she was driven by the conviction that she simply *had* to go ahead with this affair.

'The writers' group is off to Waterford for a weekend,' she announced airily, pretending to count stitches on her knitting needle as she spoke. Vera always had something on the needles, as she found it relaxing to knit while watching television. 'It was arranged at the last minute, and we voted to go this coming weekend, as it was the only one which suited everyone. Bit of a bore, really. I haven't nearly enough work done for it, and I'll have to spend the whole time making up for it, that is, *if* I go.'

'And *are* you going?' asked Brian, so used to Vera's powers of decision-making that he hardly listened to the preamble.

'I suppose I'll have to,' she said, holding one of the needles in her mouth to appear casual, and stretching out her knitting on her knee. 'Still, it should be interesting. We are only really getting down to it each time, when it is time to wrap up and go. This time we should achieve something. Had you anything in mind for the weekend, yourself?'

'Oh, I thought I'd take a bit of exercise. I've been meaning to phone some of the chaps in the agency and see would they like to stretch a leg and discuss business at the same time, maybe do Dun Laoghaire pier a couple of times, and go back to the Marine for a drink.'

They were both pretending, for Brian had no friends in the agency, either when he was there or now.

'Sounds grand. So I'll go, so ... I'll work out something food-wise so that you won't starve, and maybe you can bring someone home for lunch on either of the days.'

Brian was relieved at the thought that he would have a whole untouched weekend for himself. Maybe he *would* do something out of the ordinary, possibly invite Dorothy Reynolds around and have a second run at his 'Beyond the Grey' scheme, as their first meeting had gone quite well, and he had said that he would be in contact.

Vera nearly let out a squawk of relief. She chewed the knitting needle to keep her composure and wondered how it had been so easy. Why did things seem so difficult in advance and then turn out so simple? It was one of life's little mysteries.

An hour or so later she went upstairs and began to pack her travel bags with the items she would use over the weekend. She had treated herself to two pretty nightdresses, one with matching housecoat, some expensive toiletries and scent, and a pair of smart, strong boots with rubber soles for walking along the beach. It was bliss having her own money and being able to slip into town and get whatever she thought she might need. Normally careful with money, her spending spree was part of the new elation which kept racing through her at unexpected times, and which she was constantly keeping in check. She had met a friend in Arnott's lingerie department and felt like 'Shirley Valentine' in the film, lying to a friend that she was off to Greece to have an affair with her lover. The difference with Vera was that she *was* embarking on an affair. Into the travel bags went the new purchases, carefully folded and slipped into large freezer bags so that they wouldn't crease, and under the bed went the lot. God, it was gorgeous, looking at her new matching brown and green tartan bags, and having everything in her lingerie and cosmetic collections brought up to date at the same time. She giggled in the mirror, acting quite out of character.

The week passed quickly and Vera kept adding small items to her cache under the bed. She favoured casual but expensive clothing, and for leisure wear she bought herself a fine wool tunic in cream, under which she would wear the finest of matching silk shirts. She intended to team these with dark red leggings, and small matching red leather boots would finish off the gear. Under normal circumstances she would have thought her choice of clothes too young for her, but the sheer energy which was coursing through her these days made her suit the clothes, rather than them suiting her. A wine coloured duffel coat was just right for a warm cosy look as it was not quite spring, even though spring was her mood. For evening she chose a well cut dark brown velvet dress and matching suede court shoes. She wanted to look really elegant for Dan, who would obviously appreciate her efforts. She packed her gold and coral jewellery, which would suit the brown velvet, and with that she finished her packing list.

When Friday morning arrived she slipped her bags out into the boot of her car when Brian was in the bathroom, and set about preparing a few tasty meals for him. They had a snack lunch together and he went into town for books. Before he left she brushed a kiss on his cheek and said she would be off immediately, to get to the venue before dark. She also said that she didn't want to be disturbed unless there was an emergency, as it would spoil the enclosed feeling of the writers' weekend, but that she would check at the main Waterford post office on the Saturday, to see whether there were any messages for her, and that she would be back on Sunday anyhow. Brian said he wouldn't need the big car over the weekend and again she felt slightly guilty as she took the Rover and left him her smart little runabout. Then she closed her hall door firmly and got into the car, wheeled out the gate and settled herself comfortably, setting her face to go down to Garrycloe and start the next chapter of her life.

Dan Devereux waited for Vera to arrive. His red setter, 'Riverdance' sensed that something was afoot and was following him everywhere curiously. Dan had spent two days cleaning and polishing his home, 'The Shallows' and he had gone into Wexford to buy the best of provisions and wines. Before leaving the town he had purchased a good armful of colourful flowers, to give the house a softer look. Tidy in his habits, he thought the place had too stern an air, almost maritime, with its old brass-bound mahogany furniture, good Turkish carpets and parquet floors. He would 'jolly it up' with flowers and give it a relaxed air, as first impressions would be important. When he got back he put the flowers in large stone jars which he found in a pantry, and then he built up a fire to glowing, to give the drawing-room a friendly look.

He set about organising a meal. Dan was one of those men who regard cooking as one of life's obligations, much as having one's hair cut, or washing one's teeth, something to have done or do properly, but not something to make a fuss about. Used to looking after himself, he wanted to eat something with Vera which would be interesting, but which would require a minimum of activity at the actual time. He was really looking forward to this meal, as it was the point at which their liaison would be sealed. There were some red candles left over from Christmas, which he stuck into the silver candlesticks on the sideboard, and when he came to rest at about five o'clock he thought the effect was just right.

Dan had prepared a selection of elegant hors d'oeuvres, and matched them with country breads which he found in a small Wexford bakery. This course was to be followed by generous fillet steaks, which he would cook himself and serve with a rich mushroom and red wine sauce, along with his favourite carrots and parsnips baked in the oven with butter. Jacket potatoes would complement the main course. He also organised a cheese board with local cheeses mixed with very hard old Dutch varieties, for the mature Dutch cheeses were good for eating slowly with nuts and a basket of dried fruit, while the conversation and wine would hopefully be flowing. A red and white checked tablecloth teamed with red napkins gave a bistro effect, and Dan was pleased with the results of his efforts. He opened a rich red wine and put it near the fire to let it breathe, and chilled the Rioja which he had chosen for the first course.

On went the third Brandenburg Concerto, to allow Bach to set the mood. As he sat back and enjoyed a sherry, Dan found it hard to believe that Vera Nolan was really driving towards him, and would arrive in about half an hour. He was looking forward very much to talking and being talked to, to laughing with Vera, possibly arguing some points and to revelling in the company of a mature woman with whom he could swop some life experiences. Although he was much younger than she, he had had the breadth of activity of an older man, and he had learned much about life as he worked in different places abroad. Now, while not exactly wanting to settle down, he was ready for a relationship which would explore life. Attractive, available women of such a calibre just weren't around; either they were busy rearing their families or they were career women, and just might want to catch him and marry him before their biological clock ran down, rather than look for a deep relationship with him. Having already been married, he shied away from the idea, feeling that if he really met the right person, and they wanted one another sufficiently, it would come about naturally. For now he was content to explore a side of life he did not know, with Vera, an older woman, and one about whom he wanted to write.

During the week he had been working out the introductory chapters of his novel, starting with his life in the States, and going on to develop the story with an affair with a woman such as Vera. To his surprise the words had seemed to run off his pen. Here at home he had the perfect environment for working on his theme – thinking out his plot and giving characters to the two main protagonists whom he had based on himself and Vera – and he was rejoicing in the experience. He felt this was really coming on well, and a surge of excitement about the project was carrying him along.

He couldn't quite make up his mind whether the excitement was sexual anticipation, and felt that obviously it was, but that it was transferrable to his novel. Of course Vera's impending arrival meant that he had to lock up his writing carefully in his ship's chest, and put the key in a safe place in another room.

The dark blue Rover came slowly crunching into the drive and stopped at the Georgian door of Dan's lovely country house. Darkness was falling but Vera could see it quite well with the help of the subtle ornamental lighting in the garden. Her first reaction was typical. When she saw the gleaming yellow door between carved granite pillars and finely modelled windows in their original frame, along with the proportionately correct side wings of the house, and the rich sward of lawn disappearing into the dark, she breathed to herself: thank God Dan has plenty of class! The sea lay to the back of the house and she looked forward to exploring it over the weekend. Now as the car slowed up and stopped, she needed just that extra little bit of courage to get out of the driving seat gracefully. As she opened the car door, Dan came out of the house and towards her. He held out a hand to her and drew her up out of the car, while Riverdance circled in delight. He kissed her very gently on the cheek when she was on her feet, and introduced her to the dog who wanted to lick her hand as a greeting. He took her vanity case from her hand and put his other arm around her, leading her into the warm, wide hall.

'Welcome to "The Shallows",' he said softly, leading her into the large drawing room and over to the fire in the period marble fireplace. 'It used to be called "Wrecker's Hollow" because two centuries ago the man who owned it used to lure ships in by lantern after dark, and cause them to go aground. Then he would bring his men out to plunder the ship. No one related to me, I'm happy to say! My grandfather changed the name to "The Shallows", thinking it more appropriate to a family home.'

'It's lovely, Dan,' Vera said quietly.

'I'll get your bag from the car in a few minutes. You have to sit down now and relax with a drink for a while. Two hours' driving should be rewarded, don't you think?'

'Another reward?' she said relaxing into a large leather armchair. He bent over and kissed her gently on the lips, and then poured her a schooner of sherry. As she began to sip it, he passed her a pair of foot muffs.

'Off with your shoes.' She laughed at his practicality, wriggled her feet out of her shoes and sank them into the velvety embrace of the slippers. How gorgeous to be cherished! What had she been doing all those years, buzzing around like an off-course helicopter?

'What are you smiling at, Madame Sphinx?' asked Dan sitting back with his sherry and studying her.

69

'I'm smiling at myself, if you want to know,' she said enigmatically.

Dan found her lovely. The drive had tired her a little, lending her features repose, but her brown eyes were sparkling in the firelight and her casual clothes were perfect for the occasion. He had always admired her clear skin, and when he complimented her on it she laughed.

'No compliment, my dear. The mental hospitals are full of them – people of fifty who look nineteen!' It was a typical reply from Vera, but he liked it and rejoiced to think of the fun they would have in conversation, as well as, hopefully, in bed. Now, as the sherry made them glow, they began to loosen out and chat, and after half an hour Dan asked her to continue relaxing by the fire while he took her bags and coat from the car, and then set about serving the meal. The *Brandenburg Concerto* finished and some Scarlatti went on, and Vera sat back to allow life flow over her.

Before the meal Dan showed Vera up to a large visitor's bedroom decorated in pale yellow and white, with dressing-room and en suite bathroom. 'You'll want some space for yourself over the weekend,' he said, as he brought her into the room, and put her bags down on an oak frame. 'I'll leave you to freshen up, but first ...' He gathered her to him and pressed his face to hers. 'You can't imagine how much I am looking forward to tonight,' he breathed into her hair. 'I am longing to take you in my arms and appreciate you fully. Beyond that I cannot think. Vera, it's wonderful that you're here.' Vera felt his tweed jacket encircling her and a rush of desire passed through her.

'We'll wait until later, Dan. I want you now, but I'll be ready for you then.'

He cupped her face in his hands. 'Vera,' he said, 'Vera, Vera, Vera. Saying your name is enough to run thrills through me. You're right. We have the whole weekend ... So ... let's start with dinner.'

5

THE MEAL was great fun, the food excellent, and Dan's steaks were cooked to perfection. He had sealed them all over first, by throwing them on the hot plate of his Aga cooker to keep in the juices, and then he had transferred them to a thick frying pan. Crisp and crunchy on the outside, they were juicy, tender and quite delicious. The fresh strawberries and raspberries mixed in a liqueur and topped with cream were excellent and as Vera and he progressed from one course to another, they found themselves talking and laughing with exquisite ease, with Vera telling herself secretly that she had never felt like this before in her whole life. Then they transferred to the wide leather couch to have their coffee, and when the cups were empty, Dan took them away, and put his arm around her shoulder, taking her other hand and kissing it slowly. They sat together in the firelight, with Dan tracing her features lightly with his forefinger. The time for passion was approaching, and now he wanted to take it gently.

It grew late and Dan banked down the fire for the night, turned down the heating slightly and put on a lamp. Then he took her gently but firmly by the hand and led her up to his large front bedroom. It was decorated in three shades of pale leaf green, the darkest shade being the carpet, the middle shade the furnishing and the walls were cream, tinted with the lightest shade of the same leaf green. The furniture was old and very good. Plenty of books looked down on the room from a walnut antique bookshelf, giving it a friendly, lived-in air.

'This is where we'll spend the night, Vera. Do you like it?'
'It's perfect Dan.'
'Slip off to your own room, and when you're ready, come back to me. I'll be waiting here for you, loving the anticipa-

tion.'

Vera had never felt so elated in her whole life. She kissed him on the forehead and then went to her room and changed into one of the pretty night-dresses she had bought specially. Now she was ready for the night. When she returned, Dan was sitting on the side of the bed in cream silk pyjamas. He looked at her with a new kind of smile, a smile with hunger in it.

'Vera. Just let me hold you, let me hold you.'

She crossed the room quite unself-consciously and went straight into his strong arms. He began to kiss her passionately. She returned his kisses, and they set about making love for the first time together, with a tenderness and a strength which surprised both of them.

When Dan awoke in the morning, the sun was trying to get in under the blinds. Vera pretended to be still sleep as he slipped downstairs to prepare breakfast. He had bought locally made jams and country butter and he put them all on a tray, whistling around the sun-drenched kitchen along with the Mozart cassette he had put on for company. Vera woke when the aroma of the coffee reached the room and she went down to have a quick shower and change into the other nightdress, with its matching coat. Then she returned and waited for Dan to come up. He was still busy downstairs, letting the dog out and putting the finishing touches to the breakfast by squeezing fresh oranges into large tumblers.

Dan raised the pale blinds and let in some daylight. Vera felt as if she had walked, like Alice, through the looking-glass, and was now in a magic land.

'Breakfast, my dear,' he said, as he came into the room and put the tray down on a side table. Then he gave her a small brass-railed tray and set her up comfortably, first kissing her forehead. She felt totally natural, like a flowing liquid, with no barriers in mind or body. It was Heaven on earth. They shared the hot fresh bread and strawberry jam, and again, Dan's coffee was excellent. This man had really worked

72

out food, and knew a bit about it. He removed the tray.

'Another beautiful nightdress. I'm not letting you get dressed yet!'

Vera could have laughed out loud for no reason at all, just that she was so happy. They stayed upstairs in Dan's room making love until lunch time, and only got up to feed Riverdance. Then they dressed in outdoor clothes and took a long walk along the beach, using the little access path that ran from the back of the house to the dunes. Warmly clothed, with their arms around each other's waists like teenagers, they wandered the length of the deserted beach, sometimes saying nothing for a while, letting their minds blend, now that their bodies had done so.

Day became evening and Dan produced another dinner, this time an Indonesian meal which they set up in front of the fire, sampling all the different dishes he had prepared the day before. Some he kept warm on spirit stoves and some he slipped out and re-heated for perfect effect. They spent hours over the meal, savouring every minute of their enjoyment of it, and then they went back up to Dan's big old bed and spent another, magical night.

On the Sunday morning, Vera made the lunch, using seafood which Dan had taken out of the freezer the night before, and they sat by the fire with Riverdance at their feet until, unbelievably, it was five o'clock and time for Vera to face up to driving back home.

For Dan, the love-making had been surprising and satisfying, but for Vera it had been a voyage of discovery, of lovemaking, of Dan and of herself. She hadn't known her own resources until she delivered herself into the care of an experienced and tender lover, and she rejoiced in her new female confidence and in the belief in her own powers of attraction for a man, at a time in her life when she would have thought all that was over for most people.

'Vera, it has come to a halt, not an end.' Dan told her. 'I feel you crystalising in my mind, and I have to leave it to you

73

as to when you can come back again. Stay longer next time. Maybe mid-week. Do, do. There is so much for us to see and do.'

'Maybe I could set off for a country auction, or something like that,' said Vera. 'I'll think it out.'

'It must be soon, Vera, very soon.'

'Oh Dan, I'll do what is humanely possible. Look what you've done. You've Danned me!'

He kissed her again, searchingly.

'Don't let this go, Vera,' he said. 'It's too precious. It's been a wonderful weekend. I feel I'm twenty again, but I suppose that'll wear off. Drop me a note when you are sure you can come. If possible come next week or next weekend.'

'Who would have thought the writing course would have yielded such excitement and such fun,' Vera said. 'Of course I'll be back. I'll be back very soon, Dan Devereux. And I gather that's it, as regards the real writing course for both of us. I'm learning more from this one, I can tell you.'

'Maybe you would design this kind of course for the extra-mural studies department, Vera? Hands-on, so to speak.' They laughed and laughed as he said it.

'Goodbye, Dan.'

'Goodbye Vera.'

Riverdance wrapped himself around Vera's legs as she tried to leave, and as she drove down the gravelled drive her last view of Dan was of him lounging against one of the stone pillars in the doorway of 'The Shallows'. She knew she was leaving a part of herself behind, but what she was bringing away with her was so precious that she didn't mind. Now she had two hours ahead of her on the way home to think over the weekend, two hours to explore her affair with Dan Devereux.

Dan stood looking after the car and then he called the dog to him and went into the house. Vera's perfume was still subtly clinging to fabrics, and he loved it. He poured himself a sherry and sat by the fire listening to Beethoven for an hour or so. Then he stretched himself and had a light meal, before going upstairs and collecting the writing he had locked away.

Dan brought down the file and the disk and went along to his small study. He sat at his desk, took the cover off his computer, and started writing. He was catching, in draft form, the events of his weekend, and he was enjoying the task. As he wrote he re-lived their time together, and even felt half in love with her as his fingers tapped out his story. All facets of the weekend had been a success, particularly their love-making, and in this area Vera had surprised him. He hadn't expected her to be much of a giver, since his original impression of her had been the portrait of a calculating person, who had everything under her control. Sometimes he had aroused her slowly, not going beyond what she was ready or able to share with him, and on their last morning together, when they had woken in the big warm bed, she had made love to him quite fiercely, excitingly, aggressively, in character with her determined nature. Now he was catching these scenes on disk, and re-living his excitement and wonder, recapturing the strength of emotion, this time in words. Tomorrow he would get up really early and take Riverdance for a long walk on the strand. Then he would spend the day at the computer, re-working his draft. And there would be other weekends. There would have to be. Vera would come back many times, he knew she would, and he could depend on her to let him know by post when to expect her. For that had been their arrangement. Telephone calls were ruled out, and they would trust one another to keep their rendez-vous, when Vera would send word. When he was tired out, he put away his notes and went upstairs to sleep deeply and contentedly.

In the London School of Art a young man of eighteen named Francis Brentwood began his second week as a scholarship student. He had never really believed that he would get the bursary, and even though he had dedicated the last two years to preparing a really good portfolio, he still felt that the competition would be too much for him. His adoptive parents couldn't understand his desire to become an artist and live by his work, but they loved him, and although they weren't well off, and regretted that he wasn't training for a 'real job', they were proud of his ambition, and the tenacity which had got him, unaided, to Art College. Although he had been brought up in Manchester, Francis had chosen to train in London.

Francis had been born in London of an unmarried Irish girl, and now that he was eighteen, he wanted to do something about his great desire to find out who his mother was, and through her, discover his father also. His wish to become an artist, and his marked talent for sculpture, had made him very curious as to who had handed him down his talent and, not wanting to hurt his adoptive parents, he had decided to leave Manchester and settle in London, not only to study, but to pursue privately the knowledge he craved.

Francis was dark-haired, with pale skin and deep blue eyes, a distinctly Irish combination. He had always been different from other boys, quieter and more creative, and he became more withdrawn when, at six years of age, his parents told him that he was adopted. The shock had been tremendous, and although he did not hold it against them, he had gone around for months, staring into the faces of strangers, thinking that they might be his mother or father. Eventually calm returned and he grew used to the idea, but the deep desire was planted to find his natural parents.

Sometimes he had fantasies of being the child of hugely famous or enormously talented people, and it was his creativity that saved him from depression. He had thrown himself into the art classes at school, and, with the help of the art master, had decided to train in drawing and painting, but to make sculpture his ultimate profession. Now, he was living in London, travelling from his hostel to the college of art daily, and funded by his scholarship. For the first time in his young life he felt fully in control. He loved his adoptive parents but to find his mother, and perhaps his father, would be wonderful.

He began to paint a portrait of what he imagined his mother would have looked like about the time he was born. She would be firm faced and wide-eyed, very likely with his colouring, and she would be about the age he was now, eighteen. One day he would sculpt a head of the person he imagined. He kept his secret firmly to himself, and dreamt too, about finding an artistic father, to whom he could show his work. Then he would think that it would probably be too embarrassing for a man to meet his son for the first time, eighteen years after his birth. And would the man even know that he had a child? A pregnant Irish girl going to London to have a child might not have told the man involved, and such a man would probably have married by now and be busy rearing a family. He might not welcome the revelation that he had previously fathered a son. The idea made Francis shiver, but he returned to these imaginings time and time again. In the meantime, he had met a German girl in the art class and fallen into a light friendship, with art as the bridge. Life could have plenty of possibilities.

From the day she left the agency, Dorothy loved the sound of post dropping into her letter box in the morning. She could never resist going downstairs to scan it, and this morning it included a brown envelope from the newspaper, probably bringing a few more answers to her advertisement. She opened the envelope with the box number written on it in an ornate black script, and sat back with her coffee. At the top of the page it gave the name, address and telephone number of the sender, one Frank Donegan, an artist who enquired whether the service would extend to mounting and running an exhibition of paintings for him. The writer went on to say that he had returned from Canada a few months previously and would need help developing contacts in Ireland's art world.

Dorothy put her teacup down on her saucer with a clatter.

She read the reply again and sat back aghast. Was her past going to leap up suddenly at this, the next cross-roads in her life? It had to be the same Frank Donegan, but how could fate test her out so cruelly now, just when she was poised to start a new phase of living? She trembled a little and then realised that the choice was hers. She need never contact the writer of the letter, unless she wanted to. She now knew where this man lived, if it were the same Frank, but Dublin was big enough to avoid him, and yet small enough to meet him, if she wanted to. The choice was hers, and she could avoid the area of his address and eschew the world of art for the moment.

Frank would be about forty now, and quite likely married. Maybe she would come across him, but at this stage she felt it was better to put him out of her mind. She breathed deeply and took a sip of tea, feeling a free agent, and not someone running an obstacle course. However, conflicting feelings surged through her. Sense or sensibility? She filed the letter away carefully, promising herself that if it bothered her to have it, she would destroy it. She would show it to Kate, anyway. Suddenly a great shudder of locked-away sorrow ran through her at the thought of the baby boy she had given away for adoption. She felt sobs rising in her chest, and she let them come out. Then she went to the bathroom and bathed her eyes and prepared herself to meet the day.

Her first task was to design a public relations and advertising campaign for Brian Nolan's scheme, 'Beyond the Grey'. She worked steadily, using commercial diaries, telephoning organisations and setting up her own data bank. She liked Brian's idea, and thought that if she developed the leisure side of it, it could work well in a city like Dublin where people mixed freely, and enjoyment was high on most people's agenda. Communication of vital needs, skills and outlets would be required. The longer she worked, the more she liked the project. An older woman had once said that people should wear out, not rust, and she agreed with that idea. Now she had a vehicle for this thinking in Brian Nolan's idea of a service for older people. Both for business reasons, and because she liked the challenge of it, she intended to help him make a success of it. She was seeing a new side to a man she thought she had known well, and the new Brian was not the same man at all.

She pondered about the service they would offer. There must be a number of athletic pursuits that older people could engage in. Sychronised swimming was one which came to mind, as she liked the idea of older people being organised in something which would make them retain a pride in their bodies, and enjoy the buoyant effect of swimming. The pleasure of music and the achievement of performing simple routines would be offered. She would mention it in her initial advertising of the activities which 'Beyond the Grey' would offer. Her next objective would be to ask a designer to do a sample brochure for her and to go through it with Brian, who needed the stimulus of her professional energy to keep him working successfully. She knew plenty of people in the field who had worked for the agency at different times, and she set about contacting some of them.

Dorothy also planned to visit leisure centres in various parts of Ireland and examine the facilities, possibly arriving at agreements about special interest travel for older people. She put Frank Donegan firmly to the back of her mind for the moment.

When she reached the junction of the narrow sandy road from Dan's home and the straight road to Dublin, Vera pulled in briefly, adjusted her seat and put on a cassette of Chopin Impromptus to match her mood. She reckoned that she had until about half-past seven that evening to think back over the weekend and prepare herself to join Brian in a normal frame of mind. Then she drove on, thinking of various incidents over the three days, and sometimes involuntarily bursting out laughing. Other times a well of delight seemed to form within her, and she had to try and take her mind off her new love by thinking of work or some other subject.

She must now return home and adapt once more to Brian. Tomorrow she would have to go in as usual to work. As it was, she was behind in the necessary research work, due to her preparations for the weekend with Dan. With developments in technology racing ahead she had to keep reading up careers and studying trade magazines, in order to be able to advise the students about courses coming up in their chosen field, and keep ahead generally. Vera prided herself that she was still as bright and receptive intellectually as she had ever been, and she enjoyed her sessions in libraries around town, where all these periodicals were accessible, more for her own sake than for the sake of the students, although it was always satisfying to be in a position to give them a recommendation about something she had picked up. She had never let this side of her work slip before, but Garrycloe had put everything on hold, and she would have a busy week ahead of her.

A thought struck her. Why not work a four day week from now on and give herself more time for Dan? Offers of that kind had been made from time to time to allow young counsellors to come in on the scene. Monday to Thursday would be suitable, or possibly Tuesday to Friday, so that she would have a free Monday with which to extend a weekend, and a quiet day for returning to town. She might even be able to reduce her working week to three days, depending on what the future held.

Of one thing she was certain. She, Vera Nolan, was going on with this affair. Her body thrilled once again at the memory of the long mornings in bed with Dan, making love with the sun streaming in to hit the pale walls and the gleaming white woodwork. Breakfast in bed together had been such fun and they had discussed everything imaginable, swopping likes and dislikes. Then there had been the walk on the beach, arms around waists, with Riverdance leaping ahead. Sheer bliss. At night they had stood briefly at the window, waiting for the lighthouse beam to come around, and the very night air, with waves crashing on the strand nearby, had lent their liaison an excitement that was elemental. Dan had promised her a dawn walk the next time she came down. They would set the clock for some ungodly hour, have coffee in the warm kitchen and go out to watch the morning break over the horizon and slide over the sea. He had done some shooting of early morning flocks of geese and he said that the experience of waiting for them at that hour of day was exhilarating. How could she stop seeing such a man, when he seemed to make every minute of the day or night exciting and enjoyable? She wouldn't be called on to make any decisions yet, and Dan had been wise enough to say to her that mentions of Brian or her sons were not taboo, otherwise she would be under an unnecessary strain. He had even told her something of his unsuccessful marriage, to illustrate some point they were discussing. He seemed to face up to life as it presented itself to him, not avoiding it, nor dwelling too long on aspects of it which would interfere with positive living.

Vera hummed along with the music of Chopin and made up her mind to buy the recording of Beethoven's *Emperor Concerto* which Dan had used as background music, as they sat in silence after the dinner on the first evening. The *Emperor* would always remind her of that magical post-prandial togetherness, and their anticipation of love-making. She would definitely ask for a shorter working week, and the request would surely be accepted.

When she reached Bray at the edge of Dublin, Vera put off the music and forced her mind to change gear. What in Heaven's name would she tell Brian? She began to rehearse a fictitious report of the writers' weekend, how they had stayed in bed and breakfast accommodation in a place outside Waterford, and how they had met to discuss themes for novels. She would describe long walks and how they tried to get a feeling of the elements into their thinking. She could say that their rough drafts had shown this later on. Two jolly nights in

81

the pub would be described, as they discussed their ideas. Vera nearly believed her own imaginings by the time she reached home, and she saw that she would have to become a good liar, and that good liars need good memories.

Brian was out when she got back. This was surprising as he usually stayed in on a Sunday evening, particularly since he had retired from the agency. A note in the hall told her that he had gone to a meeting in a hotel in connection with his current project, and that she could expect him back about half-past ten or so. Well, well, well, Brian was really moving again. If he was becoming absorbed in his own life and could look after himself over a weekend easily without her, she could present her new ideas to him with less difficulty. She was delighted to have a little breathing space before he returned, time to put away her new clothes, take off her make-up and make herself look more like the original Vera. Checking out the kitchen, she saw that Brian had worked his way through the food she had left him, and she felt pleased that everything had gone well without her. She was longing to lift the phone to Dan, but determined to keep to their agreement regarding *not* phoning one another. She had said that she would jump every time the phone rang, and that there was the danger that Brian might answer, even if they had a pre-arranged time for phoning.

Then Vera rehearsed what she would say to Brian. She could say that a time had come when they both should move around more, carry on with increased energy to keep ageing at bay, see things and go places separately, undertake new interests, and all that kind of thing. Vera did a little skip around the kitchen table and then laughed out loud at herself. What was she coming to at all? She was being quite ridiculous. She sobered up and realised the importance of this first meeting with her husband since she had made love to Dan Devereux. If the affair was to continue, much would depend on how she established her new confident self at home. Vera had no plans for giving up her marriage for some time yet, and she must begin as she meant to go on, in full control.

Brian was pleased to see her when he came in. He kissed her briefly and asked her about the weekend. Vera had all her answers ready and chatted on about 'Waterford' and what she and her 'companions' had done there.

'I'll have to be allowed to read some of this writing one of these days. I'll be looking for traces of talent!' he said, good-humouredly. Vera pulled a face at him and asked him about his evening.

'Great, oh just great,' he said. 'I'm really on to something worthwhile, and to some extent I'll be working again with Dorothy Reynolds. I want to run a service for older people with energy and blood in their veins, and Dorothy has opened a public relations agency of her own and is helping me to sort out my ideas. I'll show you the outline of it tomorrow, if you like.'

'Tomorrow would be just fine,' said Vera, 'just fine, and in the meantime I want to bounce something off you. I'm think-ing of applying for a shorter working week. We had an approach by management some time back, some new scheme they were introducing to allow fledgling counsellors to have employment opportunities by giving them a day or two out of our working week, and paying them accordingly. How does it strike you as a departure?'

Dan raised his eyebrows and pursed his lips as he looked at Vera.

'It's a bit sudden, don't you think? I mean, have you thought this through, or are you acting on some impulse or other? Think about it a bit more. You know, if you give away work nowadays, you can't get it back again. It's not like pre-vious decades, and the work scene never will be like that again.'

'I've been thinking that you and I should get around more, use our lives better and have a freer feeling about our activities.'

'Do we not have that already?'

'To some extent we do, but as we both have good health and you never know how long that'll last, we should do more with ourselves. There are still lots of things *I* want to do. Antique dealing, you know the sort of thing. I'm still *only* fifty-three!'

Brian was silent. In spite of himself he was pleased with Vera's enthusiasm for taking on new interests, as it was just what he had been writing about in his project.

'Maybe you're right, Vera, but don't do anything too hastily will you?'

'I think I'll go for it. I don't want these years to slip by and find I have nothing to show for them. Anyway, a reduced working week would still mean retaining full pension rights and insurances, just salaried days unworked would be deducted.'

'Well my dear, you will do as you always do, I suppose, and that is – whatever you make up your mind to do! All the same, I imagine you are the best judge of your own situation and thanks for discussing it. At least I know how you're thinking, and what you're up to.'

Vera flinched. Thank God he doesn't, thank God he doesn't, she said inwardly. She kissed him briefly on the cheek as usual when saying good night and moved to the door.

'I'll stay downstairs for a little while,' said Brian. 'I have some papers to file and I want to re-read the notes I made at the meeting.'

Vera went upstairs to get ready for bed, this time *without* Dan Devereux. She nearly went crazy for a few minutes as she thought of Dan's arms around her, drawing her to him for the first time and then easing her gently down to lie beside him. She remembered how he had relaxed and soothed her, before arousing her to the point of union with him, and she longed with all her being to see him again. She would have to see him the following weekend as he had suggested, she simply must. She could think of nothing but Dan: Dan with his slow smile, his shrewd brown eyes, his communication and his physical energy; Dan as a lover, exploring her body for sensations; Dan as a silent companion before a glowing fire with Riverdance stretched at their feet; Dan standing in the brightly lit doorway as she drove away. Of course he must have faults, everyone did, and she would surely find them out in due course, but faults could be a focus for bonding if they were properly met and coped with, and after that magical weekend she felt he must surely be beginning to fall in love with her, although, to be honest, he hadn't said so. His very insistence on starting the affair had made her feel tremendously desired, then the conquering had been so delicious, and the cherishing had been bliss. Should she wait two weeks before returning to Garrycloe? Two weeks seemed a lifetime, but rushing things wouldn't be wise, either, and she had her new work arrangements to see to. If they went well, she would have all the more time and liberty for seeing Dan. She would have to pretend to take up another interest that would necessitate overnights away from home. She would have to get thinking about many things.

Abdul was particularly pleased with his discovery of Dorothy Reynolds, and felt she could help him develop his business in Dublin. He also wanted to open a retail outlet for fine items from Arabian cultures, and if the idea succeeded, he might open further stores in Britain, or possibly Germany. Educated in Britain, he had returned to his own country and married early, moving into his father's furnishing business in Riyadh. Spending his formative years in Britain had been exciting, and had given him great self-confidence, but when he returned to take up the threads of life in his own culture, he had felt somewhat stifled. Although he was happy with his wife and four young children, he had opted for travelling for his father's business, to escape occasionally from his own culture and taste others.

Dublin had surprised him when he had first visited it, vaguely annoyed at being snowbound in weather unusually harsh for that part of the world. The snowy conditions had persisted for three days and the airline had put him up at the Dalton Hotel for the period. He had enjoyed himself there, and the hotel staff had been friendly and competent, making a lasting impression, even though he stayed at so many hotels each year. The thoroughfares of Grafton and Dawson Streets had appealed to him, and he knew how to enjoy a whiskey in the attractive old pubs in the side streets off them. In fact, he had had a short holiday from life. He had returned a few times, when business took him to London, always staying at the Dalton for a day or two, and now he wanted to establish a business in Dublin, which maybe one of his sons could take over later on. That way he would always have a reason to visit the city which he found to be strangely relaxing. He had not taken his wife over with him on any of his visits, as he felt it might not suit her, between the four pregnancies and the fact that she was sensitive to colder climates. He found he couldn't quite describe his affinity with the place to her, for fear of offending her by enjoying something of which she was not a part. If business with Dorothy Reynolds worked out, he could be on his way to making her his anchor in Dublin.

6

FRANK DONEGAN worked out a living pattern for himself. He would spend the days in his rented studio apartment, catching the good light and preparing paintings for his spring exhibition, and the rest of the time would be devoted to getting exercise by walking the beaches and hills around Dublin. There were plenty of congenial pubs where he could spend a few hours in the evenings, bringing a book or a newspaper, and eventually he would meet people he liked. He was a stranger in his own town and this had a faint quality of adventure about it. He could have followed up connections, but he wanted to take his time and mould a lifestyle to his liking. Any solvent, apparently single man coming to live in Dublin would not lack company for long, and he didn't want to get caught up into any social sets, incurring obligations, real or imaginary. What he really wanted to do, and didn't know it, was to settle down for good.

At weekends he drove into the Wicklow hills by the old military road, built by the British in the nineteenth century to enable troops to cross the hills quickly and quell any uprisings in rebel Wicklow. He often chose Roundwood as his starting point for a long tramp across Sally Gap, where the hills were clothed in mauve and purple heather in spring and again in autumn, or across to Glenmalure where the road ends by being crossed by a river. In places, the state forestry plantations ran down to the road and the scenery was not unlike pictures from Canadian calendars. He wished he had a dog to accompany him, but his studio apartment had been chosen for work and certainly couldn't have accommodated one. Sometimes light showers swept across the hills, leaving them sparkling in the sunshine which followed them, and he often brought painting materials to catch the effect of the light. If his exhibition were to be successful, this would give him a fresh start in painting, and he could work on reproducing Ireland, after his own style. It occurred to him occasionally that it would be wonderful to have a son or daughter to go out across the hills with him, and how interesting it would be to see life all over again through a young person's eyes.

He heard nothing in response to his note to the PR consultancy and thought it as well to go ahead with arrangements in the usual way, so he dropped into one of the many galleries in Dublin, to work things out with the proprietor. He always enjoyed galleries with the life-glow of original paintings, the quietness of the atmosphere and the opportunity to see the work of other artists. He found a small one in Kilkenny Street and after one or two meetings, agreed to have his exhibition mounted there.

Pleased with himself, Frank went off to spend the evening in a pub in nearby Mervue Street, the place where many groups had begun their musical careers, and he settled into a comfortable corner with a pint of Guinness. Musicians drifted in, instruments under their arms and within half an hour or so he heard the first engaging raw sound of a bow being drawn across violin strings. A solo began and then a flute player slipped gently into the melody. The musicians played together softly until a bodhrán player began to underpin it with a rhythmic pulse. When the music came to a close, it was met by a respectful silence, followed by a burst of applause.

While Frank was following the music, two young women had come in and found places near him. Glancing at them casually, he was strangely drawn to the smaller of the two, a girl with large grey eyes, a sprinkling of freckles on a light skin, and long fair hair held back by a carved wooden clasp. She had a calm about her which he liked, and he stole a look at her from time to time. She'd be about twenty-three, he thought, and then remembered that he was forty and should be beyond spotting young women. After a while she slipped up to the musicians and spoke to one of them. He nodded and began to play his violin softly. The girl started to sing and when she had established her audience, the fiddle player left it to her voice to soar over the heads of the company as she sang *Fáinne Gheal an Lae* or *Bright Ring of Morning*. Frank was enthralled and when the girl re-joined her friend, he wished he could talk to her. Instead he enquired her name of someone close by and found that it was Doireann Ni Riordáin.

'You'll catch us all here next Sunday night,' his neighbour told him. 'Doireann usually sings here on Sundays.' Frank decided that his new interest was traditional Irish music.

Vera got her new working conditions approved without difficulty, taking a four-day week to begin with, in case she was rushing her life too much. She had to take into account that now that Brian was working from home, they could well be in each other's way if she were to be around too much. Working Tuesday to Friday would give her an extra day in her weekend and plenty of freedom. Brian went along with her change in pattern and was also secretly glad that she hadn't opted for a three-day week, as he was enjoying the privacy of his home all day, and didn't want to have to check in with Vera at various times, and lose his concentration.

He needn't have worried. Vera had a new plan, saying that she was getting bored with writing and thought that visiting country auctions would be more fun, and that she might even make a little business out of dealing in antiques. She said she would need to 'get her eye in' and acquaint herself with the trade, and could only do this by going to auctions in country houses. Vera's new low boredom threshold amused Brian, as did her logical reasons for changing horses in mid-stream, and he went along with all this without much questioning. She seemed to know what she was doing, and if she was busy and happy, that was worth everything. It would leave him free to develop on his own lines. Still, the transitition was rather abrupt, to his way of thinking.

Vera made four more visits to Garrycloe over a period of

about six weeks, and each time the tryst was pure bliss. Dan and she spent the time much as they had done on her first weekend there, as they weren't ready to venture outside the confines of 'The Shallows' and the nearby strand, and each time they plunged deeper into their relationship. She found him impossible to fall out with, as he had endless resources of balance and good-humour, whatever her mood, and he told her that he liked her when she was peeved, which made her end up by laughing, on the one occasion when she had huffed over something trivial.

Dan was making good headway with his book, and had ideas of turning it into a detective novel, with the character modelled on Vera being compromised by the discovery of a body of a man in the grounds, and her anxiety not to be found out as a lover plunging her into a dreadful dilemma. He often changed the plot, allowing himself a choice of theme, before deciding on the final format.

Vera made the same arrangements at home each time, leaving plenty of cooked food for Brian, and arriving back on either the Sunday or Monday evening, usually with some piece which she made sure to pick up in an old furniture shop, saying that she was training herself, before she stored the items in the garage. She would sell them on, anyway, she told Brian, and meantime she was learning plenty. She was indeed, but not about antiques!

One weekend she made the usual arrangements after she had made a visit to the sale at Brown Thomas, Dublin's leading fashion store, where she added a new checked jacket to her wardrobe, along with a smart, pull-down wool hat that matched the rich shade of green which was dominant in the jacket. As she got ready to go, she told herself out loud, in the bedroom, how much she was enjoying it all. Then she stopped dead, and listened to be sure that Brian wasn't nearby to hear her. She was planning to wear jodhpur type trousers, long black riding boots and the new jacket. On the night before, she said goodnight and also goodbye to Brian, as

90

she intended to leave very early next morning, when he would be asleep, and she set off around 5 a.m. to arrive in time for an early walk on the strand with Dan.

Vera skimmed down to Garrycloe in less than two hours, arriving at 'The Shallows' well before seven. There was Dan, standing on the drive waiting for her, and he looked absolutely delighted when she drove in. He pulled her out of the car and held her closely to him, the strength of his freshly showered body overpowering her. Oh, how good it was to be alive, she breathed into him silently.

'A quick coffee?' he proposed.

'I came all this way for an early morning walk, not to sit around drinking coffee!'

'And is that *all* you came for? Will you be off as swiftly as you've come?' he teased her back.

'Well, I might stay for elevenses, if I'm very well treated.' They went in for coffee and a long good morning kiss, before Dan took up her bags and locked up the car and house. It was a clear morning with pearly grey light sliding over the surface of the sea, and the very lack of headland on the horizon heightened the feeling of infinity and timelessness.

'Any chance of seeing geese?'

'They passed over at about four in the morning, if they came this way at all, but we might see a bird or two rising. There is so much wild life on the slobs in summer that it is magical coming out here in the morning, much earlier than today, of course. I'll bring you out then, see if I don't.'

Vera's heart sang at the thought of their affair lasting on through the summer and then – well, who could say? Better not to think about that now. They set off for their walk accompanied by the dog, and really stretched their legs on the firm sand, swinging along and feeling madly alive. When they returned from the beach and crossed the dunes, a car was parked there with another early morning walker preparing to get out and get moving.

'What a pity so few people get up to enjoy the day,' Vera

said grandly, as she and Dan walked by, their arms around one another.

'I don't think it would suit you at all, Ms Nolan, to have people milling around right now, or would it?'

'Oh dear, I *am* a pompous ass,' said Vera, giggling.

Back in the kitchen Dan made his favourite coffee, which he bought in cases in Dublin. When he took her new jacket from her shoulders, he buried his face in its soft collar.

'It smells of you,' he said, 'fresh and lovely. Still, I want to try you out with some sophisticated scents. I have a plan that we'll drive over to Waterford this afternoon, and try some out. I'll do the choosing if you don't mind, after all, I'm the one who'll be enjoying it.'

'So you like perfume,' said Vera, secretly delighted. 'I'll be most interested in your choice.' Then Dan took her hand and slowly led her through the house and upstairs to his bedroom. He asked her to undress him and slowly and lovingly he undressed her, before they set about celebrating their reunion.

A few hours later they showered and dressed. Then they put Riverdance into the back of the Landrover and drove in the direction of Waterford, Vera wearing large sunglasses and a headscarf, and Dan insisting on holding her hand as they went along, just like young lovers. With each mile she felt herself more and more tightly bound to this delightful man, mentally and physically. Today is only Saturday, she told herself, treasuring the thought. Today is only Saturday and we have all Sunday and Monday too. Oh, the bliss of it.

Dorothy began to carry out visits to leisure centres, working on special sporting holidays for the older person, and in this way she struck several good accommodation and activity package deals. Senior citizens in Ireland over sixty-five years of age enjoy free public transport and many of the good hotels are easily accessible by rail, so that she felt there was good business to be done off-season. Her next target was Wexford, and she booked a stay at the Tuskar Hotel, treating herself to a few days off, as well as picking up some business. She should be able to get in at least one long walk on a beach, she told herself, and she was looking forward to it.

She packed a bag of casual clothes and headed off. She sang with the radio as she drove down, taking the Enniscorthy route because it wound along the Slaney river bank, and she had time to travel slowly and enjoy it. As she breezed along in the cold fresh morning, she felt a surge of curiosity and longing for Frank Donegan. The thought of opening up the past was too much for her and she had no plans for contacting him, but she wished she could see how he had turned out, and know for certain whether or not he had married. Eighteen years is a long time in early life, and by now he would surely be settled in a world of his own and wouldn't relish his past returning. If he was the same Frank Donegan, he was the father of her child, and she would be concealing this truth from him, were she to meet him; she felt that she couldn't tell him at this stage, particularly if he were married. No, if she were not to make others suffer needlessly, she would have to keep her secret. Feeling suddenly sad, she changed the radio to a station playing cheerful popular music. She would watch for a notice of his exhibition and she might, just might, slip in and see the work, making sure first that he wasn't around. Kate had said that she would go in and reconnoitre, when Dorothy had told her about the turn in events.

Dorothy was dressed in a new track suit and trainer boots for the journey, and she looked young and full of life on arrival. She had been promised a tour of the leisure facilities at the hotel, and when she checked in, it was still quite early, so she was served a good breakfast, and then taken over the premises by the manager. Following this she retired to his office and worked on certain aspects of her project, and after a seafood lunch, she strolled along the Wexford quays looking in the antique shops, and then visited an exhibition of paintings and sculpture in the Arts Centre. There would be a play on at the theatre that evening, so she bought a ticket and then went back to the Tuskar, to lie down for an hour before dinner. Tomorrow she would set her clock early and go for a long walk on Garrycloe strand, to try it out as an added attraction. She enjoyed her evening in town very much and slept well.

The next morning dawned bright and clear with a light sea breeze coming into Wexford. It brought that indefinable but invigorating sea smell, and Dorothy felt she had chosen just the right venue for a 'Beyond the Grey' weekend. Wearing a warm hooded jacket over her track suit and a pair of ski boots she had put in for walking comfortably on the sand, she drove down to Garrycloe and parked near the dunes. She was preparing to get out of the car when a red setter dog crossed the sand, followed by a man and a woman walking closely together. She glanced briefly while they were still at a distance, and in a flash recognised Vera Nolan's distinctive features, still sufficently far away for Vera not to see her through the car window.

Then Dorothy pulled her hood forward and bent down sideways as if looking for something, to avoid being spotted. Of course she had met Vera several times down the years, at receptions and functions, but now that she was doing some work with her husband, Brian, an encounter would be disastrous. The couple passed by and walked down the sandy road by which Dorothy had come, locked in conversation and scarcely noticing her car. As there was no other car around, Dorothy surmised that they must be from a house somewhere behind the dunes.

Vera Nolan! Vera, of all people! Self-righteous Vera Nolan, with her reputation for always doing the right thing at the right time! Brian had never discussed his wife outright with Dorothy, but having taken so many telephone calls from her over the years, Dorothy knew a good deal about her personality. And here was the 'bould' Vera, having an out-of-town affair, for, quite clearly, this early morning walk on a beach had absolutely nothing to do with Brian. What a shock awaited him, if he were to find out about this liaison, and Dorothy was determined that she would have no part in enlightening him. Surprised as she was by her discovery, she felt that at the end of the day, they were all adults and must look out for themselves. She would let life run its course for herself and for others.

Dorothy only hoped that she and Vera wouldn't meet somewhere on the road through chance. What exactly was Vera up to? The man appeared attractive at a glance, taller than Vera and well-built, so they had made a handsome pair. She must be really smitten to spend a weekend away from home with him, and she had looked so youthful. Arms around waists? She laughed out loud as she drove along. Here *she* was, single and available, and there was Vera, solidly married for years and years, and off on a romantic flight. It didn't seem fair, and it certainly made her think.

What was she, Dorothy Reynolds, doing about her emotional life? Nothing. Her occasional dates with her man-friend from the North were just for fun. He'd asked her to marry him and she'd turned him down, and still they went out, because they liked one another and enjoyed the dates. But wasn't it all rather childish? Once or twice she'd come to the point of agreeing to settle down with him without a marriage commitment, but each time she just knew the depth of communication she wanted with a man wasn't there. She was probably expecting too much, and missing everything with her ideas. Why was she holding out so long, and was it that her first emotional bruising had damaged her irreparably? It had taken everything she had at the time, but it *was* years ago now, and adults had to decide to heal themselves, hadn't they? Otherwise they could go on blaming life, and let it all slip by as they did so. Was that what she was doing? Somehow seeing Vera and Dan, whatever they might be up to, made Dorothy begin to re-think her life. How about investigating Frank Donegan for a start?

A week later Frank Donegan went back to spend an evening

in the pub where the musicians gathered. He knew he'd enjoy himself there and he hoped to see Doireann again, even though he had no particular designs on her, just interested by her looks and her glorious singing voice. Maybe he would get an opportunity of speaking to her? That's what Ireland had over many other countries: you could nearly always fall into conversation with strangers, if you met them in congenial surroundings, without them feeling threatened in any way. People liked to trust, rather than mistrust one another, and traditional music seemed to form a bond between the people listening to it. He went along and found the same corner seat, and ordered his pint.

Some time later he saw Doireann coming in with a group, and as she didn't seem to be there with any man in particular, this gave him hope of contact. When he was ordering his second pint, she was at the counter and he smiled at her.

'I hope we'll hear you sing tonight. I enjoyed it very much last week.'

'Thank you. I won't be singing tonight as I have a cold, and I need my voice in good form for something next week. Maybe some other evening.'

'I'll be glad to hear you singing,' Frank said, and smiled at her as she returned to her friends. He sat there, ruminating. How pleasant it was to be able to pass someone a compliment again. He was sorely missing good female company, and he still didn't want to get involved with it. What a complex carry-on, he thought, and who'd want him anyway? Still, it was nice there in the pub, and maybe he'd meet the girl another night. At that point she looked across at him and smiled. Frank was pleased; he hadn't lost his touch after all.

The trip to Waterford was a real success. Vera and Dan strolled around the quays, watching the activity of the boats, and then gave Riverdance a good run along them, before putting him back in the Landrover, while they lunched in a pub where the prawns were so big that they nearly choked

96

them! They went shopping for perfume and tried out several kinds, before settling on a spicy scent with an Italian name, redolent of sophisticated Italy. Dan wanted to drive out to a silversmith who worked from his home outside the city, so that was their next visit, and they enjoyed themselves viewing the collection of handmade jewellery, before Dan bought Vera a dainty brooch of the theatre masks of comedy and tragedy, and chose a tie-pin in a modern swirling shape for himself. Vera could have chosen any brooch in the collection, but somehow the theatre brooch echoed her feelings of being in a real life drama, while this affair was in full course. If I ever lose Dan, I'll have this piece of theatre to remind me of Waterford with him, she told herself. She felt that the time to discuss their feelings would surely come soon, and if it didn't, then she would have to summon the courage to talk it out.

The journey back to 'The Shallows' and security was filled with the promise of the evening, and the night, and the pleasures it might bring, so they bought the ingredients for a special dinner before they left, purchasing fresh crab and lobster. Dan wanted to prepare lobster thermidor and he said he had a great wine to go with it. Vera promised him a French tarte aux fraises glazed with a suitable liqueur to give it that breath-catching flavour, and, as she was an excellent cook, she knew just the right pastry to make for it. More and more they were discovering living skills in common, and it seemed that their velvety friendship was ordained to last. As they travelled back, sitting high up in the Landrover and surveying the flat countryside, Vera could imagine herself in Kenya or somewhere in Australia with Dan, thousands of miles away, living in a world for two. We'll do that too, she promised herself.

Dan insisted that Vera dress in her brown velvet for dinner and he wore a velvet jacket himself. The meal was great fun and they played Italian music to go with the new perfume, for Dan had a real sense of occasion, and could turn anything into an event when he put his mind to it. Evening

97

became night, and magical night, with all its surprises and satisfactions, gave way to morning. They awoke to rain, but rain could not touch them in their love nest, and it made them cuddle down with no plans except spending a lazy morning together. While Dan was down seeing to breakfast, Vera suddenly thought of Brian setting off for Clarendon Street Carmelite church where they went to Mass most Sundays, where they enjoyed the choir. He would take a walk around town afterwards, weather permitting, maybe have an apéritif somewhere and a stroll in a park, before going back home. Maybe he would take in Sandymount Strand as she was away and the house would be empty, or maybe one of the boys would be back from college, as they sometimes dropped in on Sunday. Vera had scarcely had a thought for them since Dan came into her life, but as they were making their first break from home, they seemed to like it that way, and just phoned occasionally for contact. It sometimes struck Vera that everything was conspiring to allow her to have her affair with Dan. It was uncanny really, how everything was rolling back to let her through unquestioned, and she treated herself to the idea that it was surely meant to be, sketched out by destiny for her. What a relief that Brian had picked up after the first month or two of dreary isolation following his retirement! Maybe Dorothy Reynolds was the cure for all that. He certainly seemed much happier since he had started working on 'Beyond the Grey' with her. Dorothy was a reliable person and always friendly to her, so it was a bit of luck that they were in touch again, keeping Brian busy, and leaving her free to enjoy the new man in her life undetected. Just imagine, nobody knows! She hugged her secret to herself.

Dan's call from downstairs that a decent Irish breakfast was ready, and that there would be none of your Continental stuff that morning, jerked her back to life in 'The Shallows'. She begged him to give her ten minutes to get ready for it and went down to her dressing-room and slipped into the shower. Another new dressing gown and a touch of scent behind the ears put her in great form, looking forward to breakfast-ing Irish-style this time, with a good pot of tea. The music of Chopin skipped around the sparkling clean kitchen and Riverdance came over to greet her, begging her to fondle his head by turning beseeching eyes on her. Dan had everything ready, and she told him he looked the perfect man for a break-fast cereal television advertisement.

'Would you like to be the extra, coming in to enjoy it?' he asked her, laughing. 'Just imagine the effect on *le tout Dublin*, if you appeared in that ravishing house coat or dressing gown or whatever it is, to munch cereal appreciatively with me. Maybe I should join Equity and get on to one of the agencies.'

Vera loved it when Dan was giddy, as it made her giddy too, and silly ludicrous conversation sprang to her lips, quite out of character with her usual persona, as a careers counsel-lor and respectable married lady of Dublin 4.

Over breakfast Vera suddenly had the courage to discuss their affair.

'Dan, shouldn't we talk out our relationship soon?'

'Now, if you like, Vera, but for the present, anyhow, I can't see any difficulties, can you? I love our liaison or whatever you want to call it, and I don't want it to stop.'

'Not stopping means going on and on,' said Vera, deter-mined to get something firm said.

'It also means taking it as it comes, rejoicing in it and not spoiling things by introducing glum factors. You see, I have to leave it to you as to the frequency of our meetings, and hon-estly, Vera, I think you are managing everything wonderfully. I love the day before you come down. I go around the place singing.'

'But have you nothing stronger than that to say, Dan?'

'Have you? You are the one with the real live commit-ments and I can't say much more at this stage, now can I?'

Vera looked steadily at Dan and saw that he was speaking seriously. He had been thinking it through after all, she realised. She hadn't faced up to any decisions about leaving

Brian and her life in Dublin, and Dan wasn't going to help her do so. He was obviously letting things run their course, and allowing her take responsibility for herself. This man was stronger and deeper than she thought, and not so manageable either. She too would have to let the affair prove its strength.

Dan pushed the breakfast things to one side and took her hands in his.

'Vera, we're adults, and we don't have to answer to anyone but ourselves. Nor can we involve anyone, or blame anyone, or reason out our lives in ways which are not true, just to feel comfortable. All that belongs to immaturity, and hopefully we have both put that stage behind us. We have something truly wonderful together, and you know it. Let's enjoy it now, moment for moment. We'll know what to do, if a time for decision comes. Now, come upstairs and I'll find out where you put on that alluring scent.'

Vera was beaten once again.

'Dan Devereux, there's positivity and then, a layer above, there's you.'

Driving home that evening, one thought was to come back again and again to Vera's mind. It was Dan's phrase, 'We're adults, and we don't have to answer to anyone but ourselves'. It rankled because it brought with it the first tinge of guilt. He mightn't have to answer to anyone, but *she did*. She *did* have to answer to someone else, if she were staying with her marriage, because she was still enjoying the commitment of a husband and the security that went with him. She had a standard of living which resulted from Brian's many years of earning a good salary, and careful investment of it. Could she 'manage things' so that she could go on taking on all sides? Didn't some people get away with it? The Sunday newspapers were full of stories about people who apparently did. Why couldn't *she* be one of them?

Dusk had gathered and darkness would be there in a few minutes and Vera decided that it was too soon for her to become gloomy or guilty. She reminded herself once more that this affair was a brilliant, if not Heaven-sent opportunity for a woman of fifty-three, and she would be absolutely daft not to make the most of it. She switched on the car radio and gave her mind over to a concert of light music to take a rest from her thoughts.

Frank met Doireann the following week. He could see that while she enjoyed company, she wasn't trying to attract anyone in particular, and this interested him, as this was exactly what he was doing. On the way back from the counter with a drink he asked her whether she would accept one from him, and if he could sit with her for a short while. She laughed and said yes to both questions, ordering a lager. When he was settled beside her he asked her about her singing and whether she was already professional.

'I hope to be,' was the answer. 'It means everything to me, to sing professionally, full-time.'

'Tell me more. I've been in Canada for a long time and I've missed out on the phenomenal growth of interest in Irish music. Now that I'm back, I'm hearing it discussed and reading about it, and listening to it myself. Are people getting caught up with it knowlingly, or unknowingly?'

'Both. Recent television programmes focusing on traditional music have caught the attention in a big way. You see, traditional music has always been regarded as a kind of sacred trust in Ireland, and to some people's thinking, the spontaneous revival it has enjoyed in recent times may be an aesthetic risk. The commercial element is increasing and the programmes examined the question and got people talking seriously. All kinds of music have been featured.'

'Is it a question of popularity versus the traditionalists, rather than what's the best way to go?'

'It could be, and I think it is. I don't know if you follow, or even like jazz, but it came from its black roots in slavery into the mainstream of American music, and the same thing could be happening to traditional Irish.'

'And whose side would you be on if you had to answer up?'

'I'm nearer the traditionalists, but I'm twenty-two this summer, which gives me time to change.' She grinned, and then became serious. 'If I want it as my career, and I do, I'll have to be true to myself about it.'

Doireann was surprising herself at how directly she was speaking to this comparative stranger, but then she was speaking about her consuming passion. They talked on and after a while, she got up to sing. She chose an unaccompanied song in Irish, with a searching melody, and the place hushed into silence as she began. Frank was entranced. He loved every moment of it, but as she finished, he felt he didn't want to monopolise her, so when the applause died down, he thanked her for the song, and said he would be off, asking her if she would like to meet him for a drink sometime, as he got up to go. Doireann thought for a moment.

'Maybe around six some evening, because most nights I am caught up in the music scene.'

'How about this day week? Could we meet in Heneghans around six, unless you have a preference?'

'No, no. That's fine. I'll be moving off at about seven or so, so you'll understand if it's a short encounter.'

'I'll be pleased to see you, however short the time,' he said gallantly, and going back to his studio that night he felt pleased with himself. She might be only twenty-two, but she had agreed to meet him. He had no plans to push her into a sexual relationship, so the difference in their ages might make their friendship last longer, and it was a good feeling to be meeting someone for their personality and powers of communication as well as their looks. He only hoped she would keep the appointment.

7

FRANCIS BRENTWOOD worked steadily at his art course. He had few distractions and he was driven by a consuming passion to *be someone*; that determination was born of his background. He wanted to prove to himself that life's opportunities and the use of his gifts were more important than identity. He cheered himself along with the idea that identity mattered greatly, but in the end, it was how you lived your life that made you a winner. He still wondered if his artistic talent came from his father or his mother, and the better he worked, the more convinced he was that he would have to find this out. He didn't tell his girlfriend, Helga, what was on his mind, as he didn't want to breach his walls of self-defence against the world. Instead, when she told him she was going back to Germany for Easter, he planned a break in Ireland on his own. He would prepare for the trip by visiting the hospital where he had been born, to get information about his mother, if there was any to get.

The older woman in the hospital records department was kind to him and took the details. When he called later in the day by appointment, she had something for him. The dated entry read:

Patient: Dorothy Reynolds
Mother's age: 18
Nationality: Irish
Address: none given
Birth: 7 April, 1978
Weight of child: 8 lbs 5 oz.
Name given to child: Francis Oisin
Note: child given up for adoption within one week.

Next he visited the Irish embassy and got the telephone directory for Dublin. Under the name 'Reynolds' there were several references with D, but naturally no Dorothy. Anyway, Dorothy would probably have married and so he had no way of tracing her name if it were not Reynolds. It's a nice name, he thought, and would she be as nice as her name, and, if he found her, would she want to know him?

Brian noticed the great improvement in Vera's whole outlook and it occurred to him that she might well be the person to help him in his new schemes. She was the perfect example of someone entering their 'third age' in the right frame of mind, and she would look so good on a platform in all these new clothes she seemed to be acquiring. Maybe women of her age took to buying clothes to stave off the changes in their looks, but it didn't matter, one way or the other, as she looked great and she bought them out of her own money. She had adopted the right attitude to getting older with natural grace, and he had had to learn it. Indeed he could well smarten up his own wardrobe.

He set out his work for the morning. He had focused on a new area – organised study and degree courses for older people which he had heard discussed on a radio programme. 'The Third Age' was the title, and the idea enthralled him. Apparently, the Third Age movement was blossoming in Britain, where a new free university movement had taken root, and it was based on a formal French idea, where people wanting to undertake study banded together, and selected a negotiator to deal with an appointed university, to set courses for them and arrange tutors. The venue for the learning groups often rotated between members' homes, and a church or library frequently became the learning centre, once the group had settled down. The idea was a medieval one, and not only about adult education classes, for the social element was very important and the thinking was of liberation in learning, not imprisonment in it. Courses could involve walking, theatre visits, travel, computer instruction, military history, anything which could form the basis of a degree course.

Even the abbreviation of the movement appealed to him – U3A – University for the Third Age. Status, not age, had to be the qualifier and no formal qualifications were required to join a U3A group. A person had to be non-earning, that is, retired, even if they were only forty-something, and the learning groups in Britain were self-financing. Grants were available to groups, but no salaries were paid to lecturers; membership was by subscription and car pools were used for transport. Guildford and Bath had successful U3A groups, it seemed, because towns were more suitable to the system than cities, particularly industrial towns of another age, with easy movement within an area of five miles or so. Brian was convinced he could set up something similar in Dublin, Cork, Galway and Limerick, on which further groups could be modelled around the country.

Of course older people should do degree courses. What better way to hold on to the memory and retentive powers, and to use the store built up by a lifetime of reading, travelling and other activities? According to the radio programme, memory stayed intact, but it was the retrieval system that became impaired, and he wanted to find out if this could be reversed by further study. What a way to extend the span of an enjoyable and useful life. The more he thought about it, the more he realised that this was a necessary component of his service 'Beyond the Grey'. Maybe he should run an essay competition as an introduction to the scheme, and already he could think of some subjects as essay titles. And how about sponsorship?

At the onset of his work for 'Beyond the Grey', Brian had contacted 'Age Action Ireland' in Dublin and to his delight, he had found that quite a lot of research had been done, and that there were roughly 450,000 people of the category in Ireland, and eleven to twelve million in Britain. Findings revealed that people could now look forward to twenty, thirty or even forty years of satisfying life after forty, and in other areas of the world, the thinking was similar. In Australia they had 'Life-Long Learning'.

Now, Ireland was ready for 'Beyond the Grey'. He might even find a more attractive title for it!

Spring arrived and still Vera's affair ran smoothly. Brian never questioned her, except to show a mild interest in an antique piece she had acquired, for she never failed to bring back something. One day she would have to dispose of all that stuff, but she told herself that it could wait. It could wait forever, if necessary.

Dan was predictable in that he was always there waiting for her as she drove in to 'The Shallows'. If she was tense or tired, he simply put his arms around her and soothed her into good humour; he said he 'couldn't be bothered with bad humour', and that was the way to cure it. His basic positivity always won, and she loved it.

Something which had added greatly to the visits was music. In one corner of Dan's drawing room there was a small Bechstein grand piano.

'Dan, don't tell me you play the piano, as well as all your other attributes!'

'Well, I rumble a bit of jazz some evenings. I did a good classical training – we all did at the boarding school I attended, and like a lot of people I crossed over to jazz once I was no longer studying. I have to be in a certain mood for it. Funnily enough, I sometimes like to play classical music in the mornings, say, when I come back from a long walk. You play, of course?'

'Like yourself, I went through years of playing. I didn't want to devote so much time to it in those days, but that was irrelevant – you just did it. Now I'm glad I did, but really it's because I don't have the feeling that I missed out on something big. I did my Associate of the Royal Irish Academy of Music qualification, more to please my mother than myself,

106

but I'm a lapsed pianist like so many others, and I couldn't play anything right through without my music.'

'Bring your music the next time you come. We'll have a bit of fun. We might even play a few duets!'

This was the kind of reaction that Vera had grown to love from Dan. He had the gift of making the best of everything, not just skimming life, but always seeing opportunites for better quality. And of course she brought all her music down the next time she came, so that whenever it rained they had great fun playing for one another. In time they did play duets. They chose works they both knew, which Vera had found arranged for four hands in Dublin's music shops. Dan loved Bach and could still play some of the *Two-Part Inventions* perfectly. He often played his favourite, No. 8 to wake Vera, and she liked this original form of alarm clock very much. She also enjoyed Schumann and Mendelssohn, and sometimes played some of their works to Dan after dinner.

Vera still did not feel that she had reached the essence of Dan. He seemed to have a private part of his mind which was not for her, and possibly not for anyone else, and his detachment made her intensely curious. It lent their love-making a quality of mystery and made her keep looking for more, but what she was looking for was real commitment on his part, and more control on hers. Dan knew this and did not resent it. Instead it kept the relationship interesting for him, and enabled him to go on seeing Vera with anticipation. He was now deeply fond of her, but he would never love her. Instead, he needed her company, and enjoyed every minute of it. He also needed her for his book, if his creative characterisation of her were to ring true.

His novel was coming on surprisingly well. He wrote each time Vera left, while his mind was alive with her visit, and this enabled him to create other characters to balance hers. He would write and re-write, edit, add and prune, and he was faintly surprised at the strength of his conviction that this book would be published and would succeed. He had been disciplined and successful in other areas, and now this was going just as well as other projects had gone. He was flowing with the events in his life and in his writing, and Vera's obvious love for him was flattering to the ego, still sufficiently undemanding for him to go on enjoying it. She seemed to be taking her time about bringing things to a head, and as long as she was insecure, there was plenty of excitement in it for him. Her energy almost matched his, and this was terribly satisfying. Her husband, whom she rarely mentioned, must have grown a shell against her ability to control people, but now she had met her match. He told himself that until she met him, she hadn't met Rommel. Maybe the husband hadn't survived psychologically? Dan thought about that for a while, and decided to work it into the story. He also felt he was easily young enough to marry and start a family. Now that would be nice – to have children again at 'The Shallows' and experience life through them. Meanwhile the affair would have to run its course.

Vera wondered what Dan did all day. She asked him in general conversation, and he said that he was 'at a bit of a cross roads' and would have to work it all out at the end of the summer. He was thinking of running some kind of business from home, so that he could live there without getting bored, and he was studying the environment to see what would suit. Maybe deer or ostrich farming, something unusual which would attract people to visit the place and bring in an income. He said there was a market for both meat and feathers, when it came to ostriches. Vera was amused at the idea, but Dan said that the Irish climate was not unsuitable for the project. He was always full of these kind of surprises, and Vera suddenly had an unlikely vision of Brian out chasing ostriches, and tittered like a schoolgirl. When Dan wanted to know why, she simply explained that she was laughing at Riverdance's frolics!

One Friday, Vera came down after a break of three weeks, in which she had had to catch up on her career counselling. It had seemed an age since she had been with Dan, and when he took her into his arms, she couldn't wait until after dinner to make love to him. Dan knew he was fashioning another person out of the chrysalis he had met, and he had planned a real surprise for her this weekend, which would match the energy of her love making, outlandish and surprising. It also would suit the stage which they had reached in their affair.

The rain had cleared when they woke and before breakfast he handed her one of his warm dressing gowns and told her to put on her boots, not slippers. She couldn't make it out, but he still made her come downstairs with him, and he propelled her into the kitchen and out into the yard by the back door, laughing uncontrollably to himself. He guided her across the yard to one of the stable doors.

'Oh Dan, for God's sake, it's not a horse, is it? You haven't bought a horse? I told you I didn't want to ride. Oh no, Dan, now listen to me, please ...'

'No it's not a horse,' said Dan, plainly delighted with himself and his surprise, 'but you might like a ride on it all the same!' He unlocked the stable door and Vera saw a huge motorcycle parked inside.

'It's a ...' she began, and her voice trailed off.

'It's the king of the motorcycles, you goose,' he said. 'Don't you think it's brilliant?'

'Brilliant, how are you! Dan, I've never been on a motorbike in my life. What ever possessed you?'

'Look, Vera, I bought it with the two of us in mind. Two sets of gear come with it, and I thought it would be the best thing on earth for us to do a little touring, incogniti, mind, dressed in leathers and helmets. Now who on earth would recognise us in that shape?'

Vera was flabbergasted. The idea of flying around Ireland as a pillion passenger, with her arms around Dan Devereux's waist, was distinctly unnerving, but still, what a brilliant disguise! They could go anywhere they liked and never be recognised. She bent over with a sudden spasm of laughter.

109

'Dan Devereux, you will surely be the death of me, and I hope it won't be off the back of a motorbike!'

'Come on Vera, we'll blast off somewhere this morning, to get in some practice. I rode a motorbike for years in the States, and I loved it. I'd love it all the more on a bike with your arms squeezing me around the middle. Are you game?'

Beaten by his clever boxing, she replied: 'I'm game, you damned Pied Piper you! Show me the gear and I'll see if it fits me.'

Charmed with himself, Dan rolled the bike out into the yard and made her sit on the pillion in her nightdress, dressing gown and boots, so that she could imagine what it would be like. He sat at the controls and insisted she put her arms around him.

'Now,' he said. 'how do you like it?' Instantly Vera knew that she was about to love this new departure in their crazy love affair, their wonderful, zany, mad love affair.

After breakfast they tried on the gear. Vera came into Dan's room wearing it, hooting with laughter.

'Come over here, you hussy,' he said. 'I've never made love to a biker before, and now's the time.'

'I hope you haven't,' said Vera, delighted with the vision of herself in boots and zipped leathers. 'Will I leave my helmet on or take it off?'

'Vera, my deara, come herea,' was all that he needed to say.

A little time later they took out the maps and studied suitable routes. Vera packed a picnic basket, and poor Riverdance was to be severely disappointed that he wasn't included in the outing. Then they climbed on to the motorcycle and eased their way up the sandy path to the main road, and to adventure. They planned a round trip of about two hundred and fifty miles, going to Limerick and returning by Tipperary. 'If my friends could see me now' she thought, but then she had hardly any time for friends, now that Dan was the centre of her life. Pulling down her visor she set off excitedly, gradual-

110

ly getting used to balancing, with Dan instructing her about leaning in the correct direction, particularly when taking corners. After the first few miles she got the hang of it and told herself, 'If I die tonight, I'll have lived!' They rode steadily on, with the day becoming warmer, Vera safely ensconced in the big comfortable pillion seat, holding firmly on to Dan, until at last he chose a scenic spot beside a small lake to take their first break and have the picnic. He wheeled the bike into a field out of view and they spread a rug and opened the basket, exhilarated by the ride and aching for food. Vera brought out some home cooked roast beef and salad rolls, and a couple of bottles of beer, and nothing had ever tasted quite like it as they sat side by side in the field, looking like two newly arrived Martians. Vera was so happy that she almost wept.

Astride the bike once more, they sped on and on, rejoicing in their anonymity and feeling the glorious power of the machine beneath them. After a stop in a quirky but charming old pub they turned for home, taking secondary routes to try out the bike. Dan was totally in control, and their relationship seemed to be going into yet another realm. It was well into the evening when they returned to Garrycloe, and they went to their respective bathrooms to have a good soak before getting a meal together, knowing they would probably be stiff after the ride. They sat by the fire over supper, tired out and thrilled about their day, chatting it out. They still had the Monday to spend as they wished, and could do a short run if they felt like it. Dan cleared the meal away and Vera stretched out on the deep leather sofa and dozed.

Dan looked at her asleep by the fire. She was so full of courage, and not without real daring, and he admired her immensely. Lying back in an armchair with his eyes closed, he wondered how soon Vera would want to bring their relationship to a head, or whether she had decided to spin it out a bit longer. He was already half dreaming about writing a chapter about the acquisition of the motorbike, and he studied the room, and the relaxed semi-curled body of Vera in her expensive leisure clothes, and imprinted the whole scene on his mind.

The next morning they lay in bed, discussing the great excursion of the previous day. Dan still wanted Vera to do another trip that afternoon, but she only agreed to a short one, as she had to leave 'The Shallows' at about five, not to be too tired for driving. She might be carrying on like a twenty year-old, but she didn't have the same reserves of energy as she had long ago. They slipped up into Carlow on the bike, and took a more leisurely trip, this time stopping for a drink and sandwich in an out-of-the-way pub. Travelling by motorbike was a perfect arrangement, and Dan was like a boy with his first machine. He was already planning long-haul trips, with Vera meeting him somewhere, parking the car, and taking off around Donegal or Northern Ireland. Maybe they would use Derry as a starting point and do the Inishowen Peninsula!

Vera drove away supremely happy and Dan kissed her tenderly and thanked her for making the motorcycle trips such a success. He genuinely meant his gratitude, but as ever, when he went back into the house, his mind turned instantly to his novel. He gave the dog something to eat, let him out for a while, and then he ran upstairs to where he stowed his man-uscript while Vera was in the house, and brought down the latest chapters. When he was settled in to the work in his study he composed a title for the next chapter and it was *Indian Summer*, as that was what he felt Vera was experiencing in her life. He surveyed it with pride and then, for the first time, he had a twinge of guilt about her. He would certainly finish this book and hope to have it published under a pen name, for they had gone into a new dimension together on the bike and he knew it. God forbid it would be a success! He pushed away these uncomfortable thoughts and worked on busily.

Why was it always so easy to write when she was driving steadily away from him? It was the fantastic freedom he was enjoying in this affair, and the creativity which ran through him as a result. After a couple of hours' work he went back and sat by the fire watching television and having a beer with the dog lying across his feet. The cushions were still emitting the faint perfume of Vera and he put one up to his face. It would be delightful to write here, with her presence still lingering, so he planned to bring the computer into this room in the morning and work on. He could use the small strong table from the landing upstairs, and put the chess table sideways to improvise a working desk.

The following morning he took his walk, and although it was raining lightly when he set off, he enjoyed it. There was a surreal effect over the sea, with little movement in the water and a soft cloud hovering above it, mysterious and promising, and as the sun got stronger, it began to burn off, giving promise of a good day. What a blessing to live here, he thought, and Riverdance trotted beside him contentedly, sharing his mood. After a quick breakfast he sat down to write again.

Dan worked on and on. He changed his female character's name to Sally, thinking it suited her better, now that he was putting her into leather gear and bringing her as his companion on his new motorbike. Yes, it sounded sexier, and he then gave an amusing description of Sally in the new gear. The story was developing with a life of its own, and he could use the bike as a counter theme to the main thriller story.

Francis picked up his travel bag and joined the crowd queuing to get off the Ferry at Dun Laoghaire. It was about six in the morning, the air was fresh with a light easterly breeze and the sunshine played on the water. As the boat nosed inwards, the two arms of the harbour seemed to reach out and encircle him in welcome, and the yachts gleamed behind them. He could feel his spirits rising as he got ready to step on Irish ground, the first move in finding his natural mother. When he came through the gate of the new terminal he stood and gazed around him. It felt good. If he didn't find his mother

113

this time, he told himself that he would come back again and again. He was in Ireland, and involuntarily he scanned the faces of the few passers-by with interest. After breakfast in an early morning restaurant, he began to walk in the direction of the city, waiting for the buses to begin to run.

He had been reading up about Dublin in various Irish newspapers in the weeks before coming over, and he had noted the art exhibitions he wanted to view. It would be interesting to compare standards, and the Irish Museum of Modern Art was among those he marked. He also wanted to visit the Guinness Hop Store where sculpture was featured. Now he would have a chance of seeing his own work against contemporary work in Ireland. Frank Donegan's exhibition was also one of the ones he marked as being possibly worth seeing.

He caught a bus into town and then strolled along by the river Liffey to O'Connell Street. Dublin seemed to be teeming with young people. They were *everywhere*, in the cafés, in the buses, drifting about in dozens, striding by with university folders, as if Ireland had been pleasantly taken over by a bloodless coup of under twenty-fives. Suddenly he wanted to be part of this scene, and he put a visit to the National College of Art and Design higher up on his list, so that he could enquire whether he could complete his course in Dublin. It was a pleasing thought, and he then phoned home to say that he had arrived and was happily getting to know the city.

He spent the remainder of the morning in the Guinness Hop Store, studying the exhibited sculpture and had a snack nearby. Next he walked in the direction of Kilkenny Street, to see the Canadian paintings by Frank Donegan advertised in the *What's On* section of the newspaper. Two floors of the gallery were taken up by the exhibition and he liked the paintings very much indeed, impressed by the grandeur of the scenes, the bold use of colour and the sheer size of the canvases. They were much bigger in concept than anything he had seen heretofore. The artist was on duty at the desk and he thought it would be beneficial to have a word with him, and when Frank Donegan chatted to him pleasantly, Francis plucked up courage and asked him about the chances of a young painter living by his work alone. They talked for a few minutes, and then Frank had to leave.

'Drop in another day and we'll talk further about it. I'm mostly here at lunchtime.'

Before he went, Francis went back to study one of the early paintings by this artist, which was marked 'not for sale'. It was of a west of Ireland seashore, with a young girl running along the surf. It seemed to crystalise something – love and life combined. Then he left to find a hostel to check into for his stay.

The next morning was to be devoted to looking for clues to his birth-mother, so he tried to list places where he might find even the slightest trace of information. Where would he start? Suddenly the task seemed insurmountable and his first excitement died within him. He felt that she must be here somewhere in Dublin, for if he didn't believe that, he would never find her. Of course she would probably be married, and have a second family. He felt very young, very inexperienced and terribly, terribly lonely.

Vera worked out a plan by which she could bring matters to a head. She would call on Dan *à l'imprévu*. She would come a day earlier than arranged by note and see the real Dan. Would the house be as tidy as it always was when she came? Did Dan sometimes sleep late and fool around for a day? Was he ever depressed? Had he any other visitors? Surely other women had spotted him, and checked him out on some excuse or other? Had he given up the idea of writing completely? He certainly never alluded to it and when she had asked him, once or twice, he had been vague about it. The computer in his little study always had a cover on it and there hadn't been any papers lying near it, so he must have abandoned the notion. A surprise visit would surely move things on a bit.

She felt calm and in control of herself as she drove back home, along the now so familiar road, passing through the Glen of the Downs, with the hotel sparkling on the side of the Sugar Loaf mountain like a diamond brooch on a lapel. She was thinking out her future. She had quite a bit of money saved, as she had always been careful to bank her salary 'against the rainy day', and any money that had been left to her by her parents had gone straight into her account. Likewise, any that had come Brian's way, from his people, had gone into his. She could see that if she went on much longer with this dual existence, she would damage her judgment and spoil her powers of decision-making.

Vera returned home very late, as the afternoon ride on the motorbike had tired her out and she had left later than usual. She had also driven carefully, and more slowly, on account of her tiredness. Brian had gone to bed early to study something, and had fallen asleep while reading it, his glasses still on his nose, and he woke up when she was getting into the bed beside him and asked her gruffly why she was so late.

'I ran into an accident,' she replied glibly. 'The tail-back was terrible. Then I nipped out and bought something in a take-away as I was starving, but so did a lot of other people, and I had to wait a while to be served. I hope you weren't worrying.'

'As it happens, I was. I hoped you'd be all right. It's terribly late to arrive back without even phoning. You could get out for something to eat, but you never thought of phoning home, I presume. Vera, you really will have to be more considerate. Independence is one thing, but disregard of normal courtesy is quite another.' With this speech he sat back against the pillows and glared at her.

Vera was totally taken-aback that Brian might have been anxious about her. By now she had become such an accomplished liar that she had begun to believe the legends she could spin so quickly when cornered, and she thought she could deal with anything arising at home. Poor Brian, worry-

116

ing away like that, and she hadn't even given him a thought. Then the old Vera resurfaced.

'Really Brian, don't go on like that. I'm sorry I caused you anxiety, but *I* didn't cause the crash. These things happen, and not always to other people. I'm sorry.'

He turned over and affected sleep without saying 'goodnight'. Oh dear, thought Vera, is he going to become difficult just at the point when I need all my wits about me?

8

In spite of herself, Vera was beginning to think about Brian. These days he seemed to be living in a busy little world of his own, and this might be of support when she went to talk out her life with him, assuming, of course, that everything would go well with Dan, and her future with him. She now felt it was inevitable that she and Dan would sink into a shared life, and while she did not yet consider divorce as an option, she thought a legal separation would effectively take care of property, investments and moveable assets. Their sons would find it all rather shocking, and she knew they would hate the break-up of the family home, even though they might have out-grown it. She would have to write to them immediately her decision was taken, and tell them all about it. She felt a deep twinge of guilt about them at this point, but she reasoned herself out of it, saying that they really wouldn't need her from now on, and anyway Brian would probably keep the home intact, since he was now running a practice from it. There was no right way of doing it.

Brian was the deterrent to her love for Dan Devereux, and therefore he would have to go, so that her ruling passion could triumph. Of course he would suffer when she told him that she no longer wanted to go on sharing her life with him, but luckily he was so absorbed by his new practice that this might cushion the blow. In her heart she knew it wouldn't, but it was easier to see Brian as an obstacle rather than a person with feelings and emotions, whose life she had shared. She told herself she had outgrown him, and that was all that was to it.

Their friends and acquaintances wouldn't really mind that much, one way or the other, once they had got over the nine days' wonder of it. In Vera's experience, people were usually too much taken up with themselves to really mind what other people did, as long as *they* didn't get hurt.

Next morning, Vera carefully approached the question of working a shorter week than usual and leaving on Thursday instead of Friday, assuring Brian that it would be for just that week. He was extremely puzzled.

'Listen Vera, I think you're going too far with this antiques business. I know the idea is a good one, but do you have to fling yourself at every new project, the way you do? First it was creative writing, and now that's gone out the window. Now it's antiques, and I suppose that'll go the same way. You really are acting out of character, with all this independence talk. A little would have gone a long way, and God knows, I wouldn't have tried to stop you, but, I mean – five days away, wandering around looking at antiques. You'll end up losing out on your job.'

Vera took all this cautiously. Formerly, she wouldn't have been so ready to listen to a lecture, but this was quite the wrong time to start fighting with Brian, when she had to sort herself out about him, once and for all.

'I've two auctions to attend,' she said, 'and as one of them is in Carlow and the other in west Cork, I want to able to rest here and there, instead of driving all the time. I know west Cork is a good distance, but there is a tapestry collection I want to look at. I was always interested in tapestry. You know that. I dragged you off to Bayeux, that time we were in Normandy, don't you remember?'

More automatic lies. She knew that when she would come to the point of declaring all to Brian, she would feel very shabby indeed about the stream of untruths which had poured out of her all these months. Brian shrugged his shoulders. Really, Vera was becoming impossible, and it was such a pity, just when he thought she might come in on his work with him. He had been all ready to tell her that he had just landed a good contract for his services from a pension fund, and had even planned to ask her out to dinner, to celebrate the news. Very disappointing.

Vera found it easy enough to get a young counsellor to do her Thursday and Friday work for her. Monday was already arranged, so that was no problem. Then she shook off dull care and went to town, where she bought a pretty wrap-around silk dress in a colourful pattern, which would be lovely for dinner at 'The Shallows', and a pair of large earrings in exactly the same dominant colours as the dress, on the advice of the young sales woman. It was always fun to let a young person choose the accessories, because they had so much more courage, and were able to bring verve as well as elegance into the choice. Burnt-orange ski pants then caught her fancy in the leisure wear department, and to go with them she splurged on a wildly expensive soft brown sweater, and a pair of brown leather laced up boots. Looking in the changing room mirror she had to agree with the sales girl that she looked 'cool' and 'just brilliant'. The clothes would be a type of armour to help her go forward in re-planning her life.

Having ascertained that there was an auction in a country house outside Carlow, she set off via Wicklow, and found it without difficulty. She had attended auctions in Dublin over the years, and was naturally quick at spotting something interesting, so she bid for two small oil paintings of ships at sea which looked good, and got them. It was going to be exciting showing them to Dan, and seeing if he liked her taste in painting.

As soon as she was able to claim and pay for the paintings, she left the auction. She wrapped them in a large soft scarf and put them carefully on the back seat of the car and set off for Wexford, enjoying the fact that it was a lovely afternoon. She was tingling with anticipation about the surprise visit, and she drove slowly to compose herself, arriving at the village before Garrycloe towards four o'clock. She stopped for a while and refreshed herself with cologne, touched up the light make-up which she always wore for Dan, and then she set off on the last few miles, singing to the radio.

120

The gates of 'The Shallows' came into sight and it was only when she drove in that she realised that, of course, Dan wouldn't be there. He would be off shopping for her visit the next day, rustling up something really interesting for the two of them. The car was gone, and there was no sign of Riverdance, and, as she parked, she wondered whether she would wait or go in. Dan had shown her where he kept the spare key in case she ever locked herself out while he was out on the land somewhere, and after a few minutes she decided she might as well go in, and possibly do something towards getting a meal ready. She found the key under the special stone and turned it in the keyhole of the Georgian door, and then put the key back in its place.

'Hell-oooooh! Anyone at home?' There was no answer. Vera stepped down into the kitchen and peered around. Apart from crockery draining beside the sink, the place was ship-shape. Coffee had been made recently and the aroma still hung about the place, so she poured herself a cup from the percolator and heated it in the microwave. Dan's coffee had such a kick in it, and it was just the right thing after the drive. There was a box of Belgian cookies which they bought in Waterford, and she helped herself to one before she went back up to the hall, carrying her mug of coffee and finishing off the tasty morsel.

It was cool and comfortable in the drawing room with the blinds down to save the furniture from the spring sun, and she had to let her eyes become accustomed to the dim light. She looked around fondly at the room which she equated with happiness, and her eye fell on the computer which Dan had left in its new position. There were sheets of paper beside it as if he had been working there recently and, out of curios-ity, for Vera was a curious woman, she went over and picked up a page.

It was the beginning of a chapter and read: Chapter 16 – *Indian Summer*. Her heart beat a little faster as she lowered herself onto the couch and put her mug on a side table, in order to read more comfortably. She read down the first page.

> Sally looked incredible in her leathers as she stood in the bed-
> room to show them off to James. He took one look at the new
> Sally and had a wild desire to make love to her, there and then,
> although they had planned to get out on the road on the motor
> bike as soon as possible.
>
> 'Come over here, you hussy. I've never made love to a biker
> before!'
>
> 'I hope not,' was Sally's reply as he slid back the leather
> jacket, bringing her white shoulders into view. How lovely she
> looked, and how outrageously sexy for a woman of fifty-three.

Vera's hands began to shake. There were plenty more pages
for her to read. Was this a novel featuring her – and Dan – and
their love affair? It certainly read as if it was, and as the reality of the situation gripped her, she felt her heart constrict
within her. She dropped the page and rummaged through the
bundle, extracting pages here and there. She read on:

> 700 non-English-speaking Greenlanders were about to descend
> on Wexford, and no, it wasn't another international convention
> about the environment. Instead the Greenland geese were
> expected. James wanted to share the sight of Greenland geese
> flying over the Wexford slobs with Sally, and he insisted she
> come out with him one early, chilly morning, when the pearly
> grey sky stretched to the horizon, and the rough reeds slapped
> their legs as they waited for them. There they were! The geese
> were coming their way. James watched Sally's face light up at
> this new experience, the reeds swaying around them, his arms
> around her, and a glorious flight of birds breaking the silence
> with their strangled cries, and feathering the sky with their
> wings.

Vera turned back several chapters and read more. Surely she
was reading things into this script? And then she realised that
she was practising denial, one of her old life skills. She tried
again, but with each page it became plainer and plainer that
the Sally of the pages was herself. Even the physical description of the woman fitted her perfectly. Other characters
flowed in and out of the story, but each time she came on

Sally, she was coming on Vera Nolan. Then she made a supreme effort and went to the beginning. It was all about the States, until the main character, James, came back to Ireland and began to settle in. He joined a writers' group in an extramural university course, and it set the scene for Sally and James to become acquainted and slide into an affair. Page after page followed James' careful seduction of Sally, the older woman.

Vera didn't need to read any further, and a huge wave of anger and disappointment swept over her, as she put down the bundle of papers and burst out crying. Here she was, Vera Nolan, sitting on Dan's couch, after he had betrayed her in this inconceivable fashion. She had been just at the point of asking him if she could come and share his life, of breaking up her marriage for the purpose. How dare he? How could he? Was he not in love with her at all, after all the wonderful times they had together, and had their love-making had no deeper significance? The questions rushed through her mind until, with mounting panic, she realised that Dan could return at any moment, and she must now either stay and face him, or simply drive away out of his life, cutting him out of hers forever. Fight or flight? One option was as bad as the other.

Survival instinct came to her aid, and she brushed the tears away which were now falling steadily. Better go. She would *have* to go, and go quickly, but she would have to let him know that she knew of his betrayal, not with another woman, but in a glass darkly, by mirroring their affair for a purpose which completely excluded her. Would she write a note? No. What *would* she do? She would take the typescript, all of it, and she would take it because it was a story built around her, and therefore half hers. And she'd take the disk too. Where was it? Still in the computer? She pressed the little button on the front of the machine and the disk slipped out into her hand. It was simply marked *Novel* and was split into sections of roughly twenty pages, named *Novel1*, *Novel2*, *Novel3* and so on. It must be all there, but there was no time to boot up the computer to see if it was or wasn't, as Dan might drive in at any moment.

Sobbing all the time, Vera took out a mirror and combed back her hair, which had fallen into her tears. There was no point in trying to do anything with her swollen face, so she ran out to the car with the typescript and put it in her travel bag. She put the disk into a compartment of her handbag.

Then the scarf with the two little oil paintings went on top of the typescript, the paintings which she had so wanted to show Dan, and she pulled across the zip. She hurried back into the house to see if she had left anything, trembling and weeping bitterly at her own foolishness, and she took one last look at the beloved room, with the large leather sofa on which she had dozed in Dan's arms so many times. She looked across at the Bechstein and remembered that her pile of music was still there, so she stumbled across and grabbed it up, nearly knocking over a vase of flowers as she did so. It was one of the large stone jars which Dan had found in the pantry to fill with flowers for her first visit, and which they had used many times since with armfuls of greenery brought back from drives, complemented with flowers bought somewhere along the way. She crossed the hall and swung back the heavy door. It closed behind her with a sad 'clunk' and she had a fleeting memory of how Dan used to lean against the pillar each time she was driving off. With a great sob which seemed to come from the pit of her stomach, she sat into the car and put on a pair of dark glasses to hide her eyes. Vera then drove away from the house which she had thought would soon become her home.

Dan had gone to Waterford to shop for the weekend and to bring the dog to the vet to have his nails clipped. He liked the anonymity of this small city and he usually made a day of his visit, lunching at the hotel where he had been brought on treats as a child, and walking along the quays to Strongbow's castle afterwards. Today he lunched at the large modern hotel on the other side of the river, enjoying the magnificent view from the dining-room, and after lunch he went to a barber and had his hair cut smartly. Then he indulged in a work-out at a gym where he was a member, followed by a sauna. As he was expecting Vera the following day, it was pleasant to be well groomed and feel fit and trim. He did the shopping in the early afternoon, collected Riverdance and drove out to the silversmith they had visited on their trip to Waterford together. The brooch he had secretly ordered for Vera was ready. It was a hand crafted design of a large motorcycle, with two figures on it, the driver and a slightly smaller pillion passenger with arms around the driver's waist. He had ordered it by telephone, giving an exact description of his requirements, and he was mightily pleased with the result, delighted with the workmanship. He tried to imagine Vera's reaction to it and knew she would be thrilled with his ingenuity; it would make a really lovely scarf pin as well as a brooch, and be a memento of their biking trips. He took the road back to Wexford feeling in the best of humour, the dog asleep on a rug in the back seat, a cassette of Brahms booming away, and the weekend stretching before him.

It would definitely be an interesting weekend. Vera was now at the point where she would insist on working out their relationship, and this was only natural. He would let her talk it out to the end, and then he would consider, from what she had said, how he could make her see his point of view. It would depend on who would be the more courageous of the two in laying their cards on the table, and it would make a great chapter in the novel.

Dan drove down the narrow road and turned in his gate. When the car stopped, Riverdance got out sleepily and shook himself. Then he went off sniffing the gravel as if picking up a familiar scent. Dan turned his key in the door and went inside. Immediately it struck him that something was different. Someone had been in here. Doors were at different angles to the way he had left them and, of course that was it, Vera's perfume was on the air, the one he had bought her recently. My God, where *is* she, he asked himself. He called her name but there was no answer, and then he remembered that there had been no car outside, so she must have left again. How was it that she had come a day earlier than she had said? His mind flew immediately to his novel, and he rushed into the drawing room. She would surely have seen the pages lying around the computer and looked at them.

Dan's eyes flew to where the papers had been. His loose pages were gone, as were the stacked pages of his typescript, and the handwritten notes out of the wire basket. A terrible dismay filled him. Vera had been there and had seen them and taken them away with her. He put his hand down to the disk opening and it was empty. He pressed the little hasp, willing the disk to pop out, but there was none. Only then did it strike him that he had no copy on the hard drive, as it had-n't been necessary. He stood in the middle of the room, aghast at what had obviously happened, and then he went out to see if the spare key was in its usual place. It was, but at a different angle. Only Vera knew where that key was, and only Vera had been into the house.

His affair with Vera was over, that was for sure. He went out again into the hall, vainly looking for some note or message from her, but there was no note, and the only message was the disappearance of his novel. He poured himself a large whiskey and sank back into one of the armchairs. He became more and more sure, with every passing minute, that Vera would never again come to 'The Shallows', that he had been found out by her in his betrayal of her love for him, and his fondness for her. The fun they had together kept flashing through his mind, like a television trailer: the sensuous love-making, sometimes funny and generous, other times search-ing and full of discovery. He thought of all the glorious meals they had cooked and eaten together, and the music they had played for one another and as duets. Yes, the music. He got up and walked over to the table beside the piano where she had kept her pile of music separately from his, her Beethoven and Mozart sonatas, and all the Mendelssohn and Schumann pieces, some of them arranged for four hands. Then there had been her Chopin dances, the rippling Scarlatti sonatas, and the dreamy Icelandic melodies. They were all gone. Practical Vera had whipped them all up, in spite of her turmoil at her discovery.

What a terrible way for their affair to end. She must have come down a day early to surprise him, gone in, sure of a welcome and found ... found the story of her love affair with him smirkily written up, chapter for chapter, meal for meal, outing for outing, not leaving out their love-making sessions. Oh my God, he thought, what a horrible discovery for her. He was shocked into full awareness that he had been playing a game with Vera's deepest feelings; he had known it all along, but he had refused to allow it to matter to him. Now it did matter; it mattered very much indeed. Would he dare phone her and tell her so? No. He couldn't. They had made their pact about *not* phoning, and this was no time to break it. What could he expect from her in the way of understanding, anyhow? And he could not write to her either, the coward's way out of emotional upheaval.

Dan Devereux felt beaten to the ropes for the first time in his life. He was tasting real sadness now, sadness for his deliberate injury to Vera, for the loss of her company, and all the fun she brought into his solitary life, for his greed in using her primarily as novel material. He sat in a chair for a long time, and eventually heaved himself up and set about unloading the car. All the special food he had bought for the weekend was put straight into the freezer without even checking what it was. Some day he would poke through it and use it up, but not now. Then he remembered the silver brooch in his pocket and he took out the box and looked at it. There it lay, shining cheekily at him from its bed of navy velvet. He gazed at it for a few moments, thinking how it seemed to capture their wonderful secret, the woman with her head thrown back a little, holding the driver firmly about the waist, and the man bent over the handlebars. His throat tightened and his eyes began to smart with unshed tears, as he put the little box away in a drawer of his writing desk, where he could forget about it. Then he walked out on to the drive, hands in pockets, sunk in gloom, while Riverdance circled around him, sensing the change in mood and rubbing his head against his knee to comfort him.

When he got back from an extra-long tramp along the beach he had no desire to stay at home, so he put the dog in his basket and drove out into the countryside, until he found a small pub which he had never visited before. He took a seat in a corner to nurse one pint after another, and fill in the evening. Now he realised how much he had looked forward to Vera's visits. He had been staving off settling up his own life and finding worthwhile commitment in it, and he felt very juvenile about it all, and consequently very depressed. Once or twice the locals addressed him, and while he returned their greeting and made suitable remarks about the weather, he did not allow himself to be drawn into conversation. Depression had settled on him and would be with him for some time to come, and gone was the unswerving positivity which had buoyed him along since his return from the States. It was after midnight when he got back home and he went straight to bed and a deeply troubled sleep.

Each time she began to cry involuntarily, Vera could hardly see. When she checked herself in the driving mirror after some miles of journey, she looked so dreadful that she knew she couldn't go into any hotel or restaurant in that state. Here was usually-in-control Vera Nolan driving alone along the Wexford to Dublin road, bawling crying, her peace of mind quite shattered, and utterly distracted at the prospect of life without Dan Devereux. She pulled the car into the side of the road from time to time and rested, but it didn't help, and she seemed better with something to do, trying to concentrate on the road. When she was well past Gorey, she began to compose herself somewhat, for she would eventually arrive home and would need to appear normal. She would also have to make up an elaborate story as to why she had changed all her plans for an extended weekend, and was back at base in one day. Would she tell Brian that she had a thundering headache and was coming down with a viral 'flu? Not very plausible when she had left in such excellent form. Brian wasn't exactly a fool, and he was obviously beginning to resent her unpredictability after her last trip away. Better drive on, and assess the situation outside Bray. The trouble was that the nearer she came to Dublin, the greater was the likelihood of being recognised in a public place like a bar, restaurant or hotel. She couldn't stay over-night in her present condition. One look at her ravaged face and any receptionist would have dialled for back-up. Dilemma, dilemma, dilemma, and not something to which Vera Nolan was accustomed, with her carefully laid plans and dislike of changing her own decisions.

Twilight had not started, and it hadn't rained, so driving conditions were good, with not much traffic on the road. Vera even took a secondary road, thinking she would recover better without having to take other cars into account, and she drove along with her head spinning, quite unable to cope with the new turn in her life. Should she have stayed there and faced Dan with his treachery? Maybe she should, but it was a bit late for thinking that now. He would have come back at this stage and known she had been there, and he certainly would have missed his typescript and disk almost immediately, given the nature of his subject. The thought of him standing in his hall, guessing she had been there, made her burst out crying afresh. Should she have met the situation with more courage and less self-protection? She really had gone crazy in those first few minutes after her discovery of the typescript, and maybe she should have made Dan answer up about it, and even used it as a lever to fulfil her plans for him. It was so hard to know, and surely it would be a rotten base for any long-term arrangement? She didn't know, and the more she thought it out, the more confused she became. Should she turn around and drive back to Garrycloe and confront Dan with his faithlessness? She came towards a small hump-backed bridge, rummaging for another tissue in the box on the passenger seat as she approached it.

No one arriving at the scene of Vera Nolan's accident could have said what caused it, as there was no other car involved. As it was she was confronted by a hump-backed bridge with a turn directly after it, and she missed the warning sign because of her tears. She ricocheted off the wall to one side of it, coming to a halt further down the road with one side torn off the car – the driver's side. She lay in her seat, half hanging out of it, her head at a strange angle, like a dreadful 'safety first' television commercial, and when a motorist came upon her about ten minutes later, he was horrified. He set down his passenger to ensure that no oncoming motorist would plough into the scene of the crash, and sped off for help. When the Gardai and ambulance arrived, Vera was put on oxygen and brought swiftly to the nearest hospital, still alive but with serious neck and spinal injuries. Her belongings, including her zipped travel bag, were left in the possession of the Gardai for eventual delivery to her home address, details of which they found in her handbag wallet.

The pub was half-full when Frank Donegan arrived on the appointed day to meet Doireann the following week. She was there five minutes after him, which secretly pleased him, as he would have felt rather silly if he were left sitting, hoping she would come.

'Good to see you, Doireann.'

'Good to see you, Frank. Is this one of your haunts?'

'Not really. I usually frequent the pubs nearer where I live, especially when I want to hear the best traditional Irish singing available.' She smiled at the implied compliment and he ordered her a drink. 'Lager, like the last time?'

130

Soon they were sitting back with their drinks, soaking up the scene, and at ease with one another. Doireann was not talkative, but she was easy to relate to, and listened with interest to him. Frank liked her lack of artifice, and her calm assurance that the road she was choosing in life was an excellent one. It gave her a complete lack of confusion which was very attractive. While she was not assertive in manner, he sensed that there was deep determination there. Still, she would obviously have men friends, since she had accepted his invitation with grace, and had kept the appointment, so he was just a little curious as to why she had agreed to meet him, a man some eighteen years older than she. He decided to ask her.

'I need to mix around and about, and I liked your approach. Will that do?' she said, laughing. 'I don't want a so-called relationship at the moment, it's too draining emotionally and I need my adrenalin for my career.'

'And you don't regard me as any emotional risk?' It was his turn to laugh.

'You're older than me, for a start, and it's restful just to be able to exchange ideas, without any sexual challenge, which would be more predictable with someone my own age. Now, does that offend you, and if so, why?'

'As it happens, it doesn't. I think it's a good approach, and it's a pity that so much communication and companionship gets lost in relationships nowadays, with so much emphasis on sex. Am I being a boring old man already? I'm really enjoying being here with you, with the prospect of chatting and laughing. The sight of you coming through the door was delightful.'

'That's nice. We seem to understand, in the first two minutes, that no commitment is expected! Let's enjoy it.'

The time flashed by for the two of them. Eventually he asked her if she would like to meet him again, and she agreed.

'Fine, we'll do that so. I'll have the other drink you offered me and then I'll be off for a practising session with my musician mates.'

Frank ordered the beers and they discussed the music scene in Dublin, and Ireland, generally.

'Next time I'll talk to you about painting,' he said. 'I have an exhibition running at present and although I know you are a busy woman, you might find time to drop into the gallery in Kilkenny Street and have a look around. I'd like to hear what you think of my work, just as I've been telling you what I think of yours. Have you done any writing, incidentally?'

'Some poetry. It's not easy to share poetry, at least to show your own work to anyone, but maybe I'll ask you to read it. You never know!'

'When you're ready. I've done some writing too and I had a novel published in Canada, when I was moving around painting, and needed something to concentrate on in the evenings.'

The conversation roved over various topics and when Doireann got up to go, she felt she had made a new friend. For a Clare-born girl she was finding that life in Dublin was not at all disappointing.

Francis went back to see Frank Donegan in the gallery the following day. He wanted to ask whether he could do a few hours' duty for him while he was over in Dublin, which would give him a bird's eye view of Dublin's art world, and maybe earn him a few pounds towards his holiday. Uppermost in his mind was still his quest for his mother, but this would be a gratifying distraction. Frank was there, and Francis plucked up the courage to ask. It was agreed that he could do a two-hour stint over the lunch hour for the remaining week of the exhibition. This felt like success to the eighteen year-old – one day in Dublin and he had a small job in the art world.

When he took up duty, he watched the people viewing the paintings, and one day he saw a dark haired, smartly dressed woman coming in. She carefully viewed the paintings on the ground floor, standing a long time before the large work of the girl running along the strand at Achill. She seemed transfixed by it and then she recovered herself as if coming out of another world, and left quite quickly without looking around her. It was interesting how particular paintings struck people, and it was the painting he himself had picked out as special.

When his two hours were up and someone else took over from him, Francis took a train to Howth, the peninsula on the other side of Dublin Bay. He felt a great urge to paint the fishing boats tied up at the quay in the delicate afternoon light, and thought he might return the following day. He still had the art colleges to visit, as he wanted to compare his work with that of Irish students. More and more he was coming to the conclusion that this was the city where he should study, and he decided to ask Frank Donegan about it. He was now becoming quite friendly with Frank, as he had been fortunate enough to bring off the sale of a painting for him, which was a satisfaction to them both. Frank's reaction to his questions about study was that an artist thrives best where he feels at home, but that working abroad, as he had done, could bring great strengths into the work.

Francis reminded Frank of someone. He has Dorothy's colouring, he thought one day, looking at the lad working in the gallery. You don't often see the combination of black hair and dark blue eyes, he told himself, just like Dorothy so long ago. Francis asked him about the large painting of the girl in Achill which was marked 'not for sale' and Frank replied:

'I did it a long time ago and it represents a short phase in my life that I want to remember always.'

'I like it very much. I know you'll never part with it,' was what Francis said impulsively.

'I'll tell you what,' said Frank. 'If you do decide to study over here, contact me when you've fixed yourself up and I'll see what I can get for you in the way of part-time work. I'm not long back in Dublin myself, but I can ask around the galleries for you.' He paid Francis the money he owed him at the end of the week, and threw in a bonus for having helped to sell the picture. They shook hands and Francis left feeling happy that Dublin had welcomed him, if it hadn't yet revealed his mother to him. At the end of the week he returned to London and set about re-arranging his study life, with a transfer to Dublin in mind.

On his return Francis called to an adoption agency for guidance as to how he should trace his mother, but as he had been born in London and adopted there, they had no way of helping him. He was only eighteen, working completely on his own, and without any specific clues, but an insistent voice within him kept urging him to return to Dublin and live there, for that was the only way in which he could meet his mother, by coincidence or otherwise.

He told his girlfriend Helga his plans.

'Why Dublin? You haven't seen other cities, and anyway you have everything you need in London, including me!'

'I know we've been of great encouragement to one another, and if it works out, I'll bring you over to show it all to you. You'd love the traditional music they play there, as well as the other types of music, and the general atmosphere of the place. It's a young person's city.'

'But I've just got used to London. You forget that I'm German and I'm embracing a new culture as it is.'

'All the same, you'll come over to visit, and maybe stay longer. Who knows?'

By the end of the term, Francis was ready for his move to Dublin. His adoptive family let him go, giving him their blessing, as they knew it was useless to dissuade him, now that he had told them of his quest for his birth-mother. And on the morning the ferry sailed into Dun Laoghaire with him on board once more, his heart rose at the sight of the Wicklow mountains, and he felt he was coming home. He was determined that this time, however he did it, he would find Dorothy Reynolds.

Francis found a job as a waiter in a restaurant in Temple Bar, which would pay for his accommodation. The term was over, so he wouldn't be involved in students' expenses until September, and meantime he would be working in Dublin, and could look for Dorothy. When he had settled in he contacted Frank Donegan as arranged. It was good to feel that he already knew someone sympathetic to his aims.

9

BRIAN WAS working at his desk when the message came through from the police. He was desperately upset and was instantly filled with remorse, as he and Vera had not been on good terms when she left for Carlow. In fact it was the first time they had quarrelled about her new life in the world of antiques and auctions. He immediately rang Dorothy, rather than any of the family, showing himself how dependent on her he still was.

'Oh Dorothy, they say she's quite seriously injured. They think her neck is broken and there are definite spinal injuries. She's in theatre at present and her situation may be life-threatening, as she is still unconscious.' When Dorothy had expressed her upset and her sympathy with Brian, she enquired: 'Were you expecting her back this evening, Brian?'

'No, that's what's so strange. I didn't expect her back until after the weekend. I'm travelling down right away to the hospital in Wicklow where they brought her. I'll be in contact with you later.'

'Oh no, you won't, Brian, I'm coming with you, and right away. You're in shock and you're not fit to drive. I'll pick you up in fifteen minutes at your place.'

'You can't make yourself free just like that,' he said, distracted.

'I'll be round for you in less than fifteen minutes. Be waiting for me.' She grabbed her coat and handbag, took a bottle of whiskey and a glass out of the drinks cabinet and put them in a carrier bag, put on the telephone answering machine and locked up the house. When she appeared at Brian's home, he was standing on the doorstep ready for her, forlorn and shocked.

'Into the car quickly,' she said and as he seated himself, she handed him the carrier bag.

'Now pour yourself a stiff drink, sit back and let it go through you. We'll talk on the way.'

Brian did exactly as he was told and soon they were speeding out through Dun Laoghaire and on to the hospital where the Gardai had told him Vera was lying between life and death. He glanced over at Dorothy as she drove fast but carefully, concentrating on the road. What a good colleague and friend she had been to him, for so many years, and here she was again, helping him in his darkest moment. Humbled and deeply grateful, he did not talk at all but left her in peace to drive.

Brian and Dorothy were shown into the intensive care unit, where Vera was lying unconscious, her neck in a brace and various tubes coming from her body to machines monitoring her progress. Brian bent over her and whispered her name, but there was no response. The nurse signalled that he could stay with her for a while and Dorothy slipped downstairs to wait for him.

'She's stable now, but there was great anxiety about her when she was admitted. They think she'll pull through. I'll let the doctor know you're here and he'll have a talk with you.'

Brian nodded. He sat by the bed looking down on Vera's pale face. She looked much younger, and his heart smote him as he realised how far they had grown apart. Sitting sadly there, whispering her name from time to time, he longed to be back again in the early days of his marriage, when they never thought deeply about one other, but just worked satisfyingly as partners. It had all been so simple then.

The nurse called him out to see the doctor at this point. He told Brian that Vera would very probably be paralysed due to her neck and spinal injuries. He did not think there was a likelihood of her walking again, but every effort would be made to do the best for her. Rehabilitation had made enormous strides nowadays, he said. Brian wanted to weep, but he controlled himself. He had to find out as much as possible about his wife's condition while he had the opportunity.

'We'll be moving her to a major Dublin hospital tomorrow morning for special scanning, so you'll be able to monitor her progress each day, Mr Nolan. It would help greatly if you were to sit for a set period each day by her bedside, using her name and talking to her gently, when she recovers consciousness.'

Tears welled up in Brian's eyes, in spite of himself. How long had it been since he had talked gently to Vera? Maybe there was still time to recover their relationship? He would do all in his power to try, now that this strange turn in events had given him his chance to do so.

Dorothy drove Brian down to the local Garda station where they picked up Vera's bags. When they arrived back at Brian's home she came in with him to make him a cup of tea and see that he was all right for the night.

'Let me unpack Vera's bags for you Brian. Knowing men, these bags will be sitting there as full as they are today when Vera comes home from hospital, if I don't!' She was anxious to check whether there would be any clues as to Vera's activities in Wexford, and didn't want Brian upset further. He didn't protest, so she brought Vera's handbag and travel bags up to the bedroom and emptied the contents of the travel bags onto the bed. She put the cosmetics on the dressing-table, and hung up Vera's new clothes. The increase in taste and style was obvious, and Dorothy could see that Vera was dressing for this man in Wexford. She lifted out the stack of typed sheets, and put them to one side until she was finished the task, and then she turned over the bundle and flicked through the pages.

The typescript seemed to be part of a novel, and she read some paragraphs of it swiftly for a minute or two. It seemed to start in the United States, and moved on, a few chapters later, to describe a meeting between a man of about forty and an older woman of fifty-three, at a writer's group in a university extra-mural class. It also had the theme of a murder mystery. Was it the story of the affair Vera was presumably having with her Wexford friend, set in a detective novel? It looked like it. Brian had mentioned Vera's creative writing course to Dorothy, and the bits of the jigsaw were beginning to fit in; the frequent trips made by the woman to Wexford seemed to create a parallel to Vera's auction visiting trips. Were they writing a novel together? Then it struck Dorothy that the man could be writing this novel unknown to Vera, and that maybe Vera had found it and taken it. Would that be the reason for her unexpected change in arrangements? The doctor had said that her eyes were swollen, as if from crying, when she had been admitted after the crash, but Brian hadn't seemed to pick up this point.

If Brian were to come on this typescript and read it, it could well be deeply distressing for him, one way or another, as there seemed to be great love scenes in it further on. Better hurry down, or Brian would be wondering what she was doing up in the bedroom for so long. The pages were typeset on a computer, so there must be a disk somewhere. In the handbag? No disk at first glance, but when she unzipped a little pocket in the side she found it. It was simply marked *Novel*. My God, she was on target! She slipped the disk into her pocket and closed the bag. Then she bundled the typescript into one of Vera's headscarves and went downstairs carrying it.

Brian was sitting at his desk, phoning his sons to give them details of their mother's accident, and he didn't see her slip the bundle into her large handbag. She would worry about returning it to Vera some other time, now that she had it in safe keeping. She bid Brian goodnight and left, telling him that she would check on him each day for the moment, to see how he was adapting to the demands of the new situation, and when she was safely at home, Dorothy put the typescript in her wall safe.

The following morning Brian went early to the hospital to which Vera was to be transferred. He had to wait a long time while she was being examined in theatre and as he was waiting he tried to read some of the magazines he had brought along with him, but to no avail. All he could think of was the circumstances with which Vera would have to grapple, now that she was pulling through. Their whole life together would be changed, and he would have to adapt himself to it, now that she would be an invalid. But wasn't that what he had set up a service to cope with – the changes which could come about in the third stage of life? He hadn't envisaged having to carry out such a severe adaptation himself, and Vera would make many demands on him as time went on, but it swept over him how much he now really wanted to care for her, and he knew he could do it well, given a chance. Maybe through living it out he could help other people in the same situation, and guide them to still be determined to get the best out of their life. He could write about it and lecture about it, and reach others in similar situations. His work suddenly seemed valuable and relevant, and terribly important. He would be in control of it, and he vowed to himself that if Vera survived this dreadful accident, he would help her back as far as possible towards full recovery, whatever the doctors said.

When he eventually had a talk with the consultant, he was told that Vera would be in a heavy cast for some months, and the likelihood of her walking again was poor. A long period of rehabilitation and physiotherapy was needed, and all going well, she might make a good recovery in spite of her injuries. Time would tell.

Brian was then allowed in to see Vera who had recovered consciousness during the night.

'Come on old girl,' he said softly. 'It'll take time, but we are going to get you well again. You've started to pull through and I'm the man to do the pulling with you. We'll be bringing you home in time, and you mustn't worry about anything. I'm here for you Vera, and I love you. I always did, and I always will.' Vera smiled faintly at him and drifted away again. It would be some days before the reality of her situation dawned on her.

Dorothy realised that she would be able to handle things better if she read the typescript she had salvaged so carefully. If she were ever going to be able to help, she would have to be thoroughly informed.

After perusing some of it Dorothy decided that the novel was definitely written by a man. The whole tone of it, the beginning of the story in the States and the main character, who was an airline pilot, all showed a well researched story, of which the writer surely had personal experience. The style was blunt and racy, and in some places extremely funny. Within a detective story, it followed the fortunes of two people who had met in a writers' group, and fallen into an exciting, pulsating affair. It was obviously crafted by a man not without experience in the respective areas. It was well structured and she decided she might as well read as much of it as was there. The love scenes were vivid rather than explicit, dwelling on the situations leading up to them, and the reactions of the two main characters within them. In places they were quite hilarious, other times funny, tender, and occasionally overpowering. This man certainly understood women – a bit of a Tolstoy in his own way, she ruminated.

Then she came to the chapter entitled *Indian Summer* and she laughed out loud at some of the author's observations. It must be the American influence, this clipped dry humour, which burst out here and there. It was written so vividly that she could imagine herself to be the woman on the back of the bike, flying along Irish roads in disguise, and having a whale of a time. Good old Vera, was her reaction to the tale, as she read along. The nerve of her! Well done Vera, to catch the ardour of a man like this one, but oh, what a price to have had to pay for it! Who would have thought Vera Nolan had it in her? She returned to the typescript and read on until she finished all the pages. They were definitely written by a man who loved motorbikes and had good experience of them. Maybe there was more to be had on the disk? She slipped it into her own computer and brought it up under *Novel8*, the most recent section typed. As it paginated, she wondered if there would be a key to Vera's behaviour. She must have changed her mind radically, to be on a Wexford-Dublin road when she crashed the car, that was clear enough.

The new file had the heading *Countdown to the Great What Now Conference*. Yes, it dealt with 'Sally' coming to the point where an in-depth discussion was necessary for her to be able to continue with the affair. 'James' would put it to her that this was *an affair* and that turning it into a permanent liaison would serve neither of them well in the end. He decided to put great care into preparing for her visit at the weekend, so that whatever was said, or left unsaid, they would remember it as a special time together, and try not to injure one another emotionally.

The text stopped abruptly. The author, presumably Vera's lover, was just setting up his chapter, so that it would be easier to begin writing next time he sat down to do so. It was a trick Dorothy often played on herself when she was working on a long document. She tested the disk for more text, but there was none. Then she took it out of the computer and put it carefully away in a labelled cover. She stacked the loose pages in a file and called it *Novel*, and placed them both back in her safe. The man must know by now that Vera had his writings – and his disk – but it was hardly likely that he would ever come looking for them, particularly if Vera had come on them for the first time, and had left abruptly as a result. Had she come while he was out or away? Had there been a show-down? Impossible to work it out for sure, without a conversation with Vera, and that was out of the question. The main thing now was to ensure that the typescript couldn't be used to upset either Brian or Vera herself. She got up and made herself a cup of tea. Then she took out Abdul Shamir's files and got down to work on his accounts. He would be in town next week, and she wanted to have everything ready for him. As for Frank Donegan, he was far from her mind, as she settled down to her work.

Dorothy's public relations practice was going well. She had had great success with the promotion of Brian's commercial service for making life more enjoyable and profitable for older people. He was now busy fielding enquiries and organising services for interested clients, and the agency fee he charged was showing a profit, since his establishment expenses had been negligible. She seemed to have hit just the right note in her publicity material, and it was great to see his billings increasing and her percentage accordingly.

Her work for Abdul Shamir was also showing results. She had successfully launched a new range of cosmetics from the east for him, and now she was working on the opening, some months in the future, of a store in one of Dublin's more fashionable streets, in which he would sell interesting items from eastern countries, hand-picked by himself. He was paying her an excellent retaining fee at the beginning of each month so she had a cash flow to live on, and he treated her extremely well, and most professionally. He was also falling in love with her, and she knew it. She didn't want an affair with him, and she was well able to control the progress of their business relationship, but at the same time she was careful not to play around with sex, knowing that one day she might fall for him herself, if she did. He had offered her a choice of several of the exquisite eastern silks he was importing towards the venture, and although he had asked her to dine with him once or twice, she had kept meals with him to mid-day. He now came to Dublin more frequently than at the start of their collaboration and she often lunched with him and enjoyed it.

One effect this attention was having on Dorothy was the confirmation that success shared is much more satisfying than success alone, and that it was time she extended herself further and found love with someone. It seemed foolish to continue to think of Frank Donegan, but she knew he was now in Dublin, and she had seen from the papers that the exhibition she had swiftly visited had been judged a success.

One day Dorothy's curiosity got the better of her and she

went for a stroll on the street mentioned on the printed card he had sent originally, when he had answered her advertisement. Yes, his name was on the bell of the top apartment in a complex, so he probably had a studio apartment. She looked at it for a moment, and then walked briskly away, fearful that the door would open and a man would step out, in whom she would recognise the young man she had known so long ago. Was she being very foolish complicating her smooth-running life by trying to call up the past, and possibly complicating his? It felt like it.

There's a joke in Ireland that if you want to be sure of fine, hot weather for your holidays, book them for the duration of the Leaving Certificate examination. The examination takes place over a couple of weeks in June, and people often recall being roasted alive between papers, as they assessed their chances of passing, and were unable to profit by the warm weather.

Early summer that year was again hot and sunny. Off came warm clothes and on came Mediterranean colours; chairs and tables appeared outside pubs and restaurants, and within days the public parks were full of people snatching time to start a sun tan. The shops were besieged for sun and swim wear, and nobody wanted to go abroad for a sunshine holiday. Thin people began to fatten up from eating ice cream, and fat people began to thin off in the sudden warmth. Children grew inches in a few weeks, and people went around sighing 'lovely weather, but will it last?' One person who was completely oblivious to all this was Vera Nolan.

Vera lay in hospital in a plaster cast and neck support. Two of her neck verterbrae had been damaged, and skillful surgery was helping them towards healing. All going well, the cast would come off in a few months' time, but the spinal injuries seemed to be irreversible, and movement had not returned to her lower limbs.

For the first month or so after the accident, she was too ill to care about anything or anybody. Most of the time she slept under light sedation for the pain, and although Brian came every day and sat by her bed, holding her hand and saying her name softly, it was proving difficult to entice her back to wanting to live. The boys were deeply upset, having always regarded their mother and father as the constant factors in their lives, and this was the first time they were faced with the imponderable changes. Brian asked them home more, and spent time with them, something which had not occurred to him before, and although they would both be abroad for the summer gaining experience for the job market, there was a return of the family feeling, which he, and they, had thought was gone forever.

The only person who lodged in Vera's thoughts was Dan Devereux. He came and went in dream sequences and she fantasised about him, longing for and planning vaguely to see him again. Then she would recall that it was all over with him, and she would weep silently, beyond medical comfort. She must have called out his name at one stage, as one of the nurses asked Brian, 'Is Dan one of your sons?'

Brian dismissed the question, since Vera's rambling often contained the names of colleagues or students. He was so busy bonding with her in his own way that nothing else mattered to him. Within himself he encountered a new sense of well-being and self-worth, a deep peace, and he ploughed this new well of energy into his work, winning more contracts for his service.

Brian was anxious to plan Vera's eventual return home to the best of his ability. He made arrangements for professional nursing care every morning, so that Vera could be made comfortable for the day, and he fervently hoped that once home she would allow him to be her support and companion during the traumatic months to come, when she would be coming to terms with activity from a wheel chair, after a particularly dynamic and agile existence.

He was convinced that if she would help him in his work, it would be the re-making of her. She was so clever in coping with new situations, and her experience would be invaluable to others, if she could only be persuaded to pass it on. Maybe she and he would keep a diary together, and publish something worthwhile from it. After all, Vera had shown an interest in writing by going to that course of hers, although she hadn't seemed to produce anything, and had dropped it not too long after she had started it, but the scene was different now, and writing would be the perfect occupation for her.

On the practical level he worked out how he could adapt the house for Vera's benefit. He would have the back part of it converted into a top quality all year round 'garden' room, with the best of appropriate furnishing and fitments. The garden could be landscaped and re-planted, with maybe a little sculpture adroitly positioned, so that it would be a pleasure to look at during Vera's convalescence, and he would have the best advice in decorating the room for restfulness, which still included a certain amount of stimulation. He called in the suitable professionals, organised his finances, and asked that the work start immediately.

Vera was finally given a date for going home. All the time she was in hospital she had asked that she have no visitors beside Brian and her sons. In this way she could stop herself from fantasising that Dan Devereux would learn of her accident, and would fly to her bedside to declare his love for her, and insist that she go back to 'The Shallows' with him for the rest of her life. It was a silly scenario, and she knew it, but too much had happened too quickly, and she had not yet come to terms with the departure of Dan from her life, at her own instigation. The contrary forces working in her mind exhausted her, and she tried to block him out each time she found herself drifting into thinking and wondering about him, but with little success.

At the deepest level, she absolutely yearned for him. Anything would have done, a coded telephone message to the hospital, a get-well card which would make it plain that he had sent it, maybe with a picture of a large motorbike on it

– anything. She was thinking like a teenager, and she knew it, but she had travelled a long way in a short time in this love affair, and not all on a motorbike either, and she had to work through the consequences. Brian acknowledged the many kind messages that came in from family and friends, and thanked people in writing for the flowers they sent. Vera had felt unable for cards perched around the bed, roosting on the locker and flapping over the bed head, so she had asked him to keep them all safely so that she could look at them one day, and maybe get in touch with those who had sent them.

Vera wondered if Dan knew about her accident. Brian had told her that it had been carried on the *Nine O'Clock News*, and that there had been a paragraph about it in some of the daily newspapers. Dan read the papers every day, so he *must* know. At the same time she knew that it was over with Dan, over for good. When she had taken the typescript and disk, her message to him had been 'end, finis, over and out'. Where was the typescript now, she wondered warily. She asked Brian one day about her bags at the time of the crash, and he assured her not to worry, that Dorothy Reynolds had brought them back from the Garda station and had attended to them. As he made no mention of the typescript, he could hardly have seen it, and surely Dorothy would have put it away somewhere in the house when she found it among her belongings, but where? Would Brian find it? She didn't know how to tackle the matter, and she didn't want to make an exception of Dorothy and ask her to visit her in hospital, when they had never been particularly friendly. Sometimes she shrugged the question off, thinking that she was only making it important because it was her last link with Dan. Sometimes guilt seeped into her thinking, when she looked at Brian sitting beside the bed, being gentle and sweet with her, determined to make her well again and to re-build their life. Often when he was gone, she turned her face into the pillow to allow the tears flow unseen. She had left such a huge part of herself with Dan, and there was no redeeming the situation. Now the re-building of her life

147

with Brian seemed a huge task.

During the period when Vera was in hospital, Brian had acted swiftly about the garden room. It was erected quickly and the shape was semi-circular, reaching out into the garden, and measuring about fifteen feet at the longest point. A pale green and white checked floor was laid and soon an attractive glassed-in area with a ceiling rising to an artistic high point was in position. Some pieces of stained glass in stimulating colours were slipped into the windows at random points, to give an atmosphere of warmth, and outside in the garden a wonderful effect was achieved at the hands of a good landscape gardener, using the best of plants, shrubs and sculpture.

The new room would serve as Vera's day room when she came back to live at home. A system of blinds and light curtains made it cosy and welcoming when evening fell. Shelving was slipped in at different points and to one side, concealed by panelling, there was a fridge, microwave oven, drinks cabinet and small sink, with a reduced-size gas barbecue, so that, in time, Vera could entertain in a limited but efficient way. Some luxuriant potted plants around the room completed the decor, giving the look of an oasis of privacy and tranquillity. Brian got the best advice in the choice of suitable furnishing, with an orthopedic relaxing chair, low tables and attractive furniture. The existing breakfast-room nearby was converted into a pretty bedroom furnished in pale blue, with en suite bathroom where the cloakroom had been, and the new area was self-contained, with an atmosphere of space and freshness. A music system and television set were installed, and also a bookshelf, with an assortment of modern authors, who might be of interest to Vera in time. Her new quarters could only be approached through the kitchen, which would make Vera feel included in things, if she wanted to be, and ensured privacy from the rest of the house. A nurse would come each morning, and a physiotherapist would make regular visits. Lastly a cleaning firm was contracted to send someone daily, to keep the place spic and span, so that Vera wouldn't worry about that. Brian decided that he would also get help with the evening meals. In spite of all his preparations, he was apprehensive that he himself mightn't measure up to everything needed for Vera's recovery, and he knew it would be a learning process for them both.

Dorothy had worked at Brian's place occasionally over the past few months, although she now had a full-time secretary. When she was in the house one afternoon after Vera's return, she asked Brian if Vera would allow her make a short visit.

Vera was delighted to see her, although she had said that she was not nearly ready for visitors, and that she would have to work herself out first. She just had to know about the typescript, and as she had no emotional bond with Dorothy Reynolds, and no former friendship, the visit should not be too difficult. Their one bond was that they had both spent a great deal of time with the same man, Brian Nolan.

'Dorothy, you are my very first visitor!' she exclaimed as Dorothy came into her room.

'I'm honoured. How lovely it is here.'

'Pour us both a drink from the cabinet, Dorothy. I want to talk to you about something.'

'I mustn't tire you, Vera, you know that now, don't you?'

'I do, but this won't take long.' With characteristic directness, Vera started in. 'Dorothy, Brian tells me it was you who kindly brought back my bags and unpacked them for him, on the night of the accident. There was a typescript among my belongings, and I'm wondering if it went astray, either on the road, or at the Garda Station where they held my things until Brian came. I'd very much like to know where it went, and for private reasons I don't want to ask Brian about it. Can you help me at all?'

'I can, and I will,' Dorothy said, equally directly. 'That bundle of typescript was on top of your things in your travel bag, and in case it was valuable in some way, I took the liberty of bringing it home that night, and locking it in my safe, to keep it for you until the right moment came along.'

Vera was intensely relieved and didn't say anything for a moment or two. Then she looked at Dorothy over the rim of her glass.

'You will never know how grateful I am to you for doing that. God bless you, Dorothy.'

Fearing that Vera would get tired if this conversation were prolonged, Dorothy gently took the lead.

'Vera, all that matters is that your typescript is quite safe. I'll give it to you whenever you ask me for it. Maybe it's better off where it is for the moment. What do you think?'

'I think you're right. You have lifted a big weight off me without knowing it. Some day we may talk about it again.'

'Good. Now Vera, I'll just finish my very enjoyable drink and slip back to my work with Brian. I'm really privileged that you've made me your first visitor, and I just know that everything is going to go well for you. You have such determination that when you're ready to call on it, it'll be there.'

Vera smiled at her gratefully. How was it that Dorothy had the gift of knowing the right thing to say at the appropriate time? She was feeling better already. Dorothy crossed the room shortly afterwards, kissed her lightly on the cheek and left. Vera sat there quietly, released from her anxiety about the typescript. Yes, she might have enough determination to get well again ... but to walk ... well that was something else altogether. The doctors had been realistic with her about that, but she felt a wish for a second chance of life dawning on her, and, quite unexpectedly, she felt grateful to God, to Brian and to Dorothy Reynolds.

Some weeks later, Dorothy had an idea germinating, and she needed to discuss it before doing anything about it. It required an unemotional, detached appraisal and she wondered would Kate oblige her by hearing her out on it. Kate came up trumps as usual, and they arranged to meet the following evening for a meal at their favourite Temple Bar restaurant. A young waiter, new to the place, took Dorothy to her table, having checked her reservation, and what she did not know was that his heart was thumping with excitement.

When she phoned to reserve the table the evening before, the same waiter had taken the call, and when she had given the name, 'Dorothy Reynolds', he had been stunned. Dorothy Reynolds! The name that had haunted him. 'Dorothy Reynolds, so don't give our table to any other Reynolds coming in', the woman's voice had said, joking lightly.

'Thank you Madam, I'll keep a good table for you, and we'll see you around eight or so.'

Would it be she, by any possible law of chance? He had recovered himself sufficiently to take the booking politely, and he had written it into the book, his hand shaking.

Now he had posted himself for her arrival. He spoke with an English accent and when Dorothy arrived alone, he showed her to her table, asking her if she would like to look at a menu while she was waiting. Francis felt he had seen this woman before, however briefly. He wasn't quite sure, but he thought that she might have come in briefly to Frank Donegan's exhibition, and left quite quickly. The question now hammered in his brain: Was she the woman he was looking for, his birth-mother? There was no knowing, but he knew he was going to find out something about her before she left that evening, however he did it. His head was spinning, but his outward appearance was calm. Francis Brentwood was not without courage.

Kate came in almost immediately, and, having greeted one another, the two women ordered their meal from Francis, along with some Tuscan wine.

It took Dorothy some time to explain all to Kate, taking up from the point where she had seen Vera with a man in Wexford. After the Wexford visit, she had regaled her friend with the news that Vera was flying high, unknown to her husband, and they had had great fun, surmising about the Wexford love nest. Now with Vera's accident, the story had taken a very different turn.

'Kate, what do you think, taking all the circumstances into consideration? Should I put the idea to Vera that she write a novel herself, based on the man's typescript? She desperately needs something to achieve while she is recovering from this accident, and as she can't walk any longer, this would be an absorbing project for her to take on.'

'It would certainly be first-class therapy, to go through an account of the affair which has brought her into this situation, but really, Dorothy, would she be able for it?'

'I don't know, but in time I could ask her. I just want to think the idea through before even mentioning it to her.'

Kate sipped her wine. 'She must have left a large portion of herself with this man, and she really needs to get it back, if she is to recover emotionally, never mind physically. You tell me the bulk of the novel is there. Well if it were to be properly finished, taken by a publisher and skillfully edited, it could be successful, and it certainly would be a wonderful way of turning the tables on the author, and giving Vera back what she lost to him. It's some idea, Dorothy. That would let the air out of his drum.'

They sat there, laughing first, and then turning the project over in their minds from all angles. It amounted to plagiarising, if not downright theft, were Vera to take the typescript and, aided, turn it into a finished novel, but then, hadn't she been the reason for the writing of the novel? Hadn't she played the role of the main female character in it? And hadn't he stolen a great deal from her, stolen her happiness and her love? Wasn't all fair in love and war? Or was it? Maybe it was time someone stood up to him and gave him a little of what he handed out. It was far too soon to say anything to Vera. Vera hadn't discussed her affair at the time of asking Dorothy about the typescript, but Dorothy loved to do her homework in advance of a situation, and this is what she and Kate were doing now.

'Kate, Vera has taken such a beating, that this could be the emotional healing of her. She always had a certain toughness and it can't have gone away, it must be lying dormant ready to re-assert itself. I doubt if she has literary talent, or it would have shown itself by now, but she *is* a finisher when she starts something, even if she seems to have flunked on that writing course. That was different. Something very much stronger was calling, to put it mildly! Now, what do you think?'

'Yes the bulk of the work is done, the tone is set, and the resolution of the story still remains to be worked out. Maybe we could get someone to work on it with Vera. But there's the question of Brian. He should never know who was taking the star role in the novel, particularly now, when he is walking in seventh Heaven! We'll have to work that side of it out, certainly.'

'Going back to the main idea. Do you think I should wait for some time before doing anything about it? Vera did say that she would tell me the full story some day, and if she does, that would be the perfect time to do it.'

'Yes, you should wait. I think it's a brilliant idea, Dorothy. Vera's husband wouldn't need to know. It's surprising how little people *need* to know. Most of the time people say too much, and upset one another unnecessarily, and often unconsciously. In fact, the project would be all off if there was any danger of his knowing about Vera and her affair. The fat would be in the ointment then! We'll get around it somehow, if it ever goes ahead.'

'All Vera would need would be a computer and printer to begin with, and I'd love helping her,' said Dorothy smiling contentedly. The idea was taking shape and she was enjoying herself.

'I think it would be a scream,' Kate finally said, and the two of them fell across the table laughing at the idea of neatly turning the tables on the man whom they didn't even know, but felt they did.

'He deserves it, even if he's a lovable demon, and if he's anything like the lead man in his typescript, he'll be able to take it.'

They lifted their glasses to the conclusion they had reached, as they had done at the end of chats down the years, and then they passed to other subjects until it was time to go. Kate went to the ladies' room to freshen up after the meal, and Dorothy beckoned to the young waiter to bring her the bill.

Dorothy paid it, leaving a generous tip for the lad, a good-looking young fellow and certainly extremely attentive, who had looked after them well without invading them at the meal.

'Madam, we sometimes serve special meals here, ethnic dishes and celebration menus. If you are interested and would like to give us your card, we would send you on details from time to time. We do it as a promotion for the restaurant. We'd be glad to have you on our circulation list.' He sounded so earnest and polite that Dorothy was won over by him.

'Well, it sounds a great idea. I'll give you my card.' Dorothy opened her handbag and took out a card, which she handed to Francis.

'Thank you *so* much,' he said a little breathlessly and hurried to the back of the restaurant. Nice lad, Dorothy thought again and then Kate re-joined her and they strolled out into the early summer night.

Francis' hand trembled as he held the precious card Dorothy had given him. He knew he shouldn't have made up that story about the promotion, but he *had* to get this woman's address somehow. If only she would turn out to be his mother. She had black wavy hair like his, and she had the same colour blue eyes and pale skin. Was he jumping to wild conclusions? He quickly concealed the card in his pocket and hurried back on to the restaurant floor. It wouldn't do to lose his job, and no one must know he had obtained a card from a client under false pretences. He tried to put his excitement out of his mind, by concentrating firmly on the other diners in the restaurant for the remainder of the evening. Tomorrow he would work it out whether it would be better to write to this

woman, or to telephone her. He would have to persuade
Dorothy to see him.

10

$V_{\text{ERA GREW}}$ to love her garden room, and as she improved slightly in general health, she appreciated it all the more. She was enormously grateful to Brian for his effective action in getting it ready for her, and he glowed in her appreciation. She was finding it gradually easier to relate to him, considering she had practically ceased doing so altogether before her accident. Sitting in her orthopaedic chair each morning she sized up her situation and vowed anew that she would make the best of it. It was almost like a religious vow, as she was finding it desperately hard to think forward and not backwards; she only thought for one day at a time, and she allowed Brian be good to her, while she was still missing Dan very much.

Each day Brian wheeled Vera into other rooms when she asked him, so that she wouldn't feel too enclosed, but she always ended up by wanting to go back to the room in which she found peace, her own special room. When the nurse left mid-morning she arranged to have a private hour in which she would not be disturbed under any circumstances, for she needed to be alone for a guaranteed period each day, to get control of her thoughts. This was her own time and Brian respected it utterly, only asking her to use her bell if she needed him. Vera also planned to use this time to psyche herself up to trying to stand, if not walk. Each day she screwed up her courage, and each day she made a tiny bit of progress. No one must know until she had taken her first step again.

Vera had no worries about the household. A woman came in daily to serve a light lunch and to prepare a dinner which could be heated up when required, and the house was kept spotlessly clean by the cleaners. All laundry was sent out.

Some weeks later Dorothy asked Brian if she could see

Vera again. The medical reports had been good, and Vera immediately sent a message that she would welcome a visit from her. Dorothy had it in mind to present her project before Vera settled into a reasonably normal life, whatever that would be, for what Dorothy had in mind would require great dedication and patience, and couldn't be fitted in with any other undertakings. She would not mention it unless Vera gave her an obvious opening.

Brian went out briefly and Dorothy was left alone with Vera. She was delighted when she saw Vera looking so much stronger. Although the cast and brace had been removed, Vera's legs were still paralysed, and the prognosis for movement in them was very poor. She avoided discussing her condition where possible.

'Vera you look so much better. This is great,' Dorothy greeted her.

'I feel infinitely better and now I go in and out of the garden in my chair, whenever I feel cabin fever coming on,' Vera said smiling. 'How are you, Dorothy? It's a pleasure to see you again, it really is.' Her personality seemed to be mellowing, and she had a new self-worth earned through her personal courage, with no immediate urge to dominate the conversation.

They chatted on, and sipped a soft drink, enjoying the garden view, with everything blooming outside.

Suddenly, Vera gave Dorothy the opening she required.

'What I need now is something to do. I need some kind of project which wouldn't involve mobility, but which would be well worth doing. I don't mean hand-work, tapestry and that sort of thing, pleasurable though it can be. I need something interesting to think about. I find great solace in looking at the garden growing prettier every day, but I don't know, I'll just have to find something to *do*. I need to achieve something big! It may sound silly, but I just know that that's the sort of thing to bring me on quickly. Do you understand, Dorothy?'

Dorothy grasped the opportunity so fortuitously offered

to her.

'Vera,' she said, taking a sip from her drink, 'I understand. And I think I may have just the project for you.'

Dorothy was counting on Vera's inner toughness which would enable her to do anything she really set her mind to achieve, and by now she had no misgivings about what she was on the point of suggesting. The moment was right. She sat back in the large cushioned chair and said, 'May I?' as she slipped her feet up on the foot stool.

'You have? How do you mean? What kind of a project, Dorothy?'

'Believe me Vera, I've thought this one out, and I was only waiting until you would be well enough to discuss it. You can use a computer or word processor, can't you?'

'Yes, I can. We used them to file and update the information we required for career guidance and counselling. I don't know whether using one would put a strain on this old neck of mine, but why do you ask?'

'I think we can launch you as a first-book author under a pen name,' Dorothy said levelly. She felt it was the time to lay all the cards on the table, if she was going to be able to help this woman back to recovery, and Vera had already made progress. It was a daring plan, but Vera might be persuaded to adopt it, and come out of this situation winning.

'Look Dorothy, I've never written anything. Do you mean you want me to write up what it's like to have a serious accident? Sure nobody would want to read that except a doctor.'

'I mean you could edit and finish the typescript you brought back from Wexford.'

Vera looked at her astonished.

'Yes, Vera, I read it. I had to, to know what to do with it, and I'm glad I did, otherwise I wouldn't have kept it safely away from everybody else. You'll have to forgive me, but the alternative was having Brian find it and read it. Once I had recognised who was playing the lead female role, that thought was just too awful.'

158

Vera nodded slowly, feeling Dorothy had acted correctly, and she was grateful to her for doing so.

'It's all right, Dorothy. You did the right thing in the circumstances.'

'Vera, it's *your* story, isn't it?'

'Yes, it is. That's what caused the accident. I came down to visit Dan Devereux a day earlier than arranged – that's his name by the way – and when I went into the house, I found the typescript. I was so upset when I realised that he really only wanted me as a role model for a novel, after all the wonderful times we had together, that I grabbed it up, and the disk too, and I drove away roaring crying. My mind was on anything but the road and I never saw the turn at that bridge. I don't remember anything after that, but you could say that I was heading for a crash, in more ways than one.'

'Maybe so. Vera, I know this idea is outrageous, but I also know that this is *your* story. Why shouldn't you re-write it from the typescript? It's well written and very funny in parts. I think we could do it together, if you worked on it first, chapter by chapter. I would try and find the right person to finish it. If it were taken on by a publisher, it would be professionally edited before being actually published. You know, Vera, you'd get back a great deal of what you probably think you've lost, if you did this, a big part of yourself! Think about it.'

Vera was dumbfounded at the audacity of the proposal. It would be plagiarism at it lowest, but she would be re-writing her own story. Now where did that leave a person? Dorothy was silent as Vera absorbed the import of her suggestion.

'Dorothy, I've been lying backwards and forwards to Brian for months, pretending I was interested in antiques professionally, and letting on that I've had to visit auctions all over the place, in order to have an excuse to stay out of Dublin each time I visited Dan.'

'He did mention auctions to me, and I could see he never questioned the new interest in things antique.'

'Yes, of course, I did visit a few places, and I bought small

159

items from time to time, but the whole caper was a cover up for my visits to Garrycloe.'

'Vera, tell me that you'd never be tempted to confess all to Brian. Now promise you won't. That would be the worst thing possible for him.'

'No, Dorothy, I don't intend to indulge myself at his expense.'

'You must think me dreadful, lecturing you like this. He's *your* husband and I shouldn't be telling you how to act with him. I'm so relieved you've no notion of telling him. Now listen, Vera, I've a confession to make too. I was in Wexford one weekend, on business, and I got up early to have a walk on Garrycloe strand. I saw you there with a man, coming back from your walk!'

'Oh my God, the woman in the car, parked just where we were coming over the dunes!'

'I hid my face from you, of course,' Dorothy said, laughing. 'Now wouldn't it have been a disaster at that stage, if you had recognised me?'

The two women looked at one another for a moment, holding back the desire to laugh out loud, and then they shrieked and howled with laughter. It rang through the room, and it was fortunate that Brian wasn't in the house to come in and ask what was going on. As they mopped their eyes and recovered their composure, they forged a bond which would never be broken.

'You don't get away with anything in this world,' said Dorothy. 'Sooner or later, the bill comes in. The miracle of it all is that we survive from day to day so well. Someone I know used to say that we get from day to day, barely avoiding disaster! Now, Vera, I've probably exhausted you, but I've given you something to think about. Rest assured that your secret will go to the grave with me, unless you want it otherwise, and if you want that typescript back to work on it, just ask me and I'll come running.' She got up and gave Vera a light hug which was warmly returned.

Vera sat quietly after Dorothy had gone. The laughter she had shared with her had acted as a healing balm, and she felt herself to be the possessor of a new emotional balance. Yes, she would get well, and probably faster than the doctors expected. Now she could feel herself wanting a second chance in life, and once again she felt immensely grateful to God, to Brian and to Dorothy.

Frank Donegan got down to serious painting once again, rather than slide into a lazy drive. His exhibition had been very successful and he had sold well, so that he was recognised as a painter to be reckoned with in the Dublin world of art. To ward off the easy life, he stocked up on paints, bought several large canvases and cleared out any rubbish in his studio, in order to start work.

He wanted to capture something of Ireland, something which had not been painted to death, and that was the Midlands area. He was interested by the great semi-circular skies over the vast brown bogs with their frieze of burnt orange ferns, the clear skies after showers, and the black clumps of stacked sods here and there. The loneliness of the bogs attracted him, and he felt extremely happy on the walks he had taken around Ferbane in County Offaly, where the brown land stretched to the pale skies, and the pinky-beige stony roads picked their way across its surface. Clumps of bog cotton would break the mass in the summer, and he wanted to go down there and make this countryside his own, with great bold strokes of brown and black, relieved here and there by sharply coloured images and huge dappled, metalised skies. It seemed urgent to him now to capture the immensity of the scenes he encountered in the Midlands. The forlorn cries of the curlew seemed perfect for the moods he experienced, and he decided that paintings done here would form the basis of his next exhibition.

Frank had been much impressed by the work of Thomas Hart Benton, the Missouri painter who had left the New York art world to put the real America on canvas. He just loved the vigour of Benton's work, and he aspired to mural painting on the scale that Benton had. He had felt empathy with this artist and his concept – get a grand design and then go and paint it. He loved the idea that an artist is a man applying his work to life, catching it, mirroring it, and Benton's search for beauty intrigued him. It might be a beaten-up steam boat, but Benton contended that there isn't beauty without fulfilled needs, and a boat which had served its time was beauty to him. Now Frank wanted to introduce figures involved in needed occupations, people on the land, old men relaxing in a bar, the wisdom in a work-worn woman's face, a young musician observed playing the flute. The idea excited him immensely. He thought he might get Doireann to take a break from her music and come down with him for a few days. Maybe she could bring some new material she was working on, and he could catch her on canvas, practicing her unaccompanied singing, out where no one but the curlews would hear her. He'd ask her next time they met.

Vera took about a week to make up her mind about Dorothy's proposal. She knew that she had no literary talent and would need help, and she regarded the proposal as a rather dreadful one, to calmly take someone else's work and pass it off as her own, but then, she had lost so much through this man. Her love had been thrown back at her unwittingly by Dan, and she had lost her health and mobility. Gone was the magic of the affair which had sustained her emotionally for months, and gone too was the chance of ever seeing the Dan she still loved, in spite of herself.

What did she have? She had a devoted husband who was trying, to the best of his ability, to bring them together again in friendship. She had a lovely home, and she could recover gradually, without stress. She allowed herself a few minutes of sadness, for the old Vera would have to go if a new one were to emerge, strong and brave, from this whole experi-

162

ence. She still had some mourning to do, before she could concentrate on anything actually outside of herself, such as the
diversion of her counselling skills towards older people,
which Brian had touched on lightly one evening. It was quite
a good idea, to switch her experience to servicing the 'third
age', and she would need some months of training in order to
be able to contribute properly, but she wasn't nearly ready
yet, for anything so organised. If she took up Dorothy's proposal and worked through Dan's typescript, that would be
therapy indeed. It would allow her to go through the whole
experience, and if a publisher were to accept the finished
work, there would be something at the end of it. For the first
time since the accident she felt a little quiver of excitement run
through her, and she liked the feeling. No, she wasn't dead
yet!

One morning after she had worked on her secret resolve
to walk again, trying to balance and push one foot forward in
the strictest privacy, she thought: I'll re-write the typescript,
and that will strengthen my determination to walk again. It's
the same thrust after all, pushing the human being beyond its
accepted limitations. I'll do it, and I may succeed in achieving
both, some day.

She phoned Dorothy.

'Dorothy, I'll do it.' she said simply. 'I'll work through it,
and then we'll have to get someone who writes well to work
on it with me. Hang the consequences. Dan Devereux will
never sue me for plagiarising. He wouldn't do that. We once
had a great bond, and he wouldn't dishonour it. There is no
malice in him, I'm convinced of that. Expediency was his
forte, but then, it can be mine too!'

Dan Devereux did know about Vera's accident. The television
news had carried a brief mention of it, but as he had been in
an out-of-the-way pub until closing time he had missed it. It
was the following day, when he was reading his newspaper
that he came on a paragraph in a late column saying that Vera

163

Nolan, travelling back to Dublin, had a serious car accident. He was appalled, and he knew just how upset she would have been, and what would have upset her. He was racked with guilt for the first time in his life.

Dan worked out different schemes by which he could contact Vera, or at least let her know how badly he felt about it, but in his heart he knew this was useless, and would only contribute to her misfortune. As he sat trying to read the paper in his little study, he knew it would be a long time before he re-gained full peace of mind. Work would be the only answer.

Dan had been serious when he mentioned ostrich farming to Vera, and now he got in contact with a farm in the south of Ireland, which the Department of Agriculture and Food had told him was carrying on the business successfully. He planned to go down to Cork and visit it.

The fun had completely gone out of the motor bike for him, and although he could have made the trip by bike, it now seemed aimless and somewhat juvenile, to speed around the countryside just for the hell of it. He took the Landrover instead.

He locked up 'The Shallows' and put Riverdance's basket in the boot, so that he could bring the dog with him for company and let it sleep in the jeep overnight. As he took the scenic road which runs beside the Blackwater river for many miles across Counties Waterford and Cork, he was poignantly aware of the beauty of nature around him. The dark, steady river bubbled up in light froth here and there, where the fish were showing themselves, and the effect was like the top of a creamy pint of Guinness. The trees laced themselves in a pattern overhead and the morning air was fresh, carrying the smell of burning turf now and then as they passed isolated cottages. There was now no point in wishing he could share any of this with Vera ever again. Not only was she gone, but she could well be lying injured in a hospital bed, and all because of him. Had she crashed because she was crying, he wondered? If she had lost her emotional control, that would certainly have affected her driving, for Vera was a good steady driver and certainly wouldn't have been speeding. There was nothing he could do to find her and come to rest about her.

Dan lunched at a well-known restaurant in east Cork, having first given Riverdance a good run on nearby Ballycotton strand. He could have bought fish fresh from the trawlers there, but now it didn't seem important, the way it had done when Vera was in his life. He strolled around the gardens of the restaurant, inspecting the splendid range of fresh herbs, and tasting tiny exquisite tomatoes in the greenhouses. The sheer atmosphere and restfulness, allied to the low profile and continuous industry going on at the place, made him make up his mind to make a success of 'The Shallows', whatever path he took for its development.

The visit to the ostrich farm was interesting, and the large comical birds were a definite attraction for visitors. People came here all throughout the summer, it seemed. The whole breeding process was explained to him and he began to consider it seriously. He had plenty of land behind the house, if he wanted to fence it off in pens and erect suitable buildings, and as he liked getting up early with a purpose, he felt sure his industry and care would be well rewarded. He also had it in mind to breed a small amount of interesting sheep such as the Jacob-type with their multi-coloured fleece, and beyond that he had a hazy notion of having a large aviary. Peacocks would be out of the question, as Riverdance would never tolerate them, but if the animals and birds were correctly fenced in there would be no problem. Dan also had plans for bringing overseas visitors shooting on the mud flats outside Wexford in the winter months, and he was building up a good supply of licensed guns for organising the sport. He felt he must keep occupied the whole time, and the trip down to Cork gave him new structures on which to work over the summer, although he would not find any inner peace for months to come, and thinking about Vera caused him a surprising amount of pain.

'Dorothy, have you a moment to listen to me, it's Vera Nolan.'

'You sound so excited, Vera. What is it?'

'My computer was installed this morning and I find I'm able to work on it without pain. You can't you imagine what it's like, having done nothing at all since the accident. Now for the real news. I'll start work on the typescript and see how I get on.'

'Vera, you're a marvel. I can't tell you how delighted I am.'

'God knows how it will turn out, but if I remember rightly, there is a great deal of it done. I'll call you in for consultation when I've done the first chapter. The only thing now is that I need the typescript, so could you be an angel and plan a visit, bringing it with you? Soon? I've told Brian I'd like to work on something with you, and if he wouldn't mind, I don't want to discuss it. He was so pleased to see me fired with enthusiasm about anything, that he didn't care one way or the other. It wouldn't do to hurt him, in any case.'

Dorothy smiled to herself and shook her head at the thought of all the times Vera had risked hurting Brian during her affair with Dan, and how she had been obviously planning to give him a death blow by leaving him. How quickly the human being accommodates to new circumstances and feelings, and can shed the past and its implications. Maybe it's just as well, she mused.

'I'll drop you over the typescript this evening, along with something to read. Just be sure and tell Brian that I'm coming over, and everything will go smoothly, Vera. Full marks for courage.'

11

F<small>RANCIS</small> B<small>RENTWOOD</small> went home that night from the restaurant in high excitement. He couldn't understand why he was so convinced that this woman was his natural mother, when there must be many other people to be contacted in the course of such a search. He didn't sleep, as he weighed up whether to write to Dorothy or telephone her, now that he had her address and telephone number. Instead he made himself a cup of tea in the early hours of the morning and came to the conclusion that phoning would be better, because if she didn't answer his letter, he would be left in an agony of suspense. If he phoned, at least he would know her reaction, and whether or not she would grant him an interview. After all, she had been kind about giving her card, and she had left him a good tip.

He thought it best to phone early, say about nine o'clock in the morning, when he might catch Dorothy at her work. He asked permission to use the house phone where he was staying, and then settled himself in an armchair in the sitting-room. After a moment or two spent getting his courage together, he dialled.

'Dorothy Reynolds and Associates,' said the voice of the woman he had served the night before.

'Hello, this is Francis Brentwood speaking. I am the waiter who looked after you in the Studio restaurant yesterday evening, Ms Reynolds. I expect you are surprised at my phoning you.'

'Well, yes, I am. What is it, Francis?'

Dorothy thought that maybe she had left something in the restaurant.

Francis plunged in. 'Ms Reynolds, I think we might be related, and I am wondering if you would be good enough to meet me, to see if, in fact, we are?'

'Tell me more, please,' said Dorothy.

'I know it is asking a lot of you, but you see, I'm looking for a woman called Dorothy Reynolds because that was the name of my birth-mother. I'm an adopted child.'

Dorothy stalled in amazement.

'Yes, that's my name, of course. But why do you think there might be some connection between us?'

'Well, it would be a start for me, if I could talk to you, and perhaps you have relations of the same name, something I could work on?'

Dorothy sat back, amazed. Could this be her own son talking to her? The boy of about eighteen, with colouring like her own? The picture of him fell into place as she sat holding the receiver. Yes, it could be, but still, it wasn't necessarily so. Recovering slightly she replied: 'Yes, of course we can meet.'

'You can't imagine how grateful I would be. I should explain that I am at art college, and I'm working at the restaurant to keep myself in funds.'

'We could meet somewhere pleasant, say in a hotel. Do you know the Dalton on St Stephen's Green? There's a comfortable tea room off the lobby and we could have a chat there in privacy.'

'Can we meet some day soon, Ms Reynolds? I have to come on duty at the restaurant at about four each afternoon, so could it possibly be some morning?'

Dorothy still hadn't committed herself about Francis' reason for wanting to meet her, giving herself space to manoeuvre, but already her pulse was racing with excitement.

'Let's make it the day after tomorrow, then, say at eleven o'clock in the morning in the Dalton, if that suits you. I have things to do in town and it would be no trouble for me to drop in there then.'

'Oh thank you for being so nice about it. I'll be there, watching out for you.' They said goodbye and Francis sat back in the armchair, emotionally exhausted, the receiver still in his hand. Would she really turn out to be his mother? And if she did, would she accept him as her son? Questions raced through his mind so fast, that in order to gain some control he went upstairs and took a cold shower, to shock himself into normality and calm his nervous system. Then he went down town to divert his thinking from this exciting development in his life.

Dorothy also collapsed back into her chair. She had been busy working on a promotion when the call came through, and now all thoughts of work had fled her mind. Could this boy really be her son? She knew young people could have fixations about tracing a natural parent, and could even be obsessive about it, so she must take this young man along carefully. If he *were* her son, would he expect to join her in her life here in Dublin? And who had reared him, and how would they react to the new situation? Her heart beat fast, and her throat filled up at the possibility of the miracle that her son had found her.

Francis had said that he was an art student. Then her thoughts flew to Frank Donegan, an artist by profession and the father of the child she had given up. Was this mere coincidence, or was there such a thing as coincidence anyway? If he were Frank's son, wouldn't she have to tell the boy this, and let him go after him, himself? It all seemed to be closing in on her, and Dorothy's mind whirled at the possibilities involved. Frank could be married at this stage and not in a position to acknowledge and welcome a son into his life. She was thinking too far ahead, she told herself.

Two days later it was time to go and meet Francis. Dorothy had thought of nothing else since Francis' call, and she felt it was better to see the boy and assess the whole situation.

At eleven that morning she entered the hotel, sure that Francis would be there before her. He was there, sitting in the lounge, where he had been composing himself for some time, and he jumped up nervously when she came in.

'How are you, today?' she began pleasantly, shaking

inwardly at what would now have to be discussed.

'Oh, I'm very well, thank you. I'm so glad you've come,' he said, all in one breath.

'Let's order some tea then,' she said, matter of factly, 'and we'll get down to talking right away.'

'I have a confession to make, and I must make it now,' he said piteously, seeing his happiness slip away from him.

'What is it, Francis?'

'I made up that story about promotions in the restaurant. I just had to find out where you lived, so that I could contact you, I had to.' His eyes filled with tears.

'Francis, it's all right. Don't worry at all about that. Of course you had to do something, and in the little time you had, I think you did rather well!'

Francis breathed a huge sigh of relief. He resumed. 'You see, as I said on the telephone, I'm looking for my natural mother, my birth-mother. I was born in London and adopted when I was a week old. My mother had your name, and I made up my mind to come over here to Dublin and try and find her. Although my adoptive parents have always loved me and have been very good to me, I had this driving force to come and see if I could find her. Then when you came to the restaurant, I just thought it might be you, and I couldn't stop myself contacting you. Do you mind awfully?'

'No, Francis. Let's piece this together.'

'Ms Reynolds, I have a copy of my birth certificate with me. May I show it to you?' He carefully pulled the certificate out of a leather cover, which he was carrying in an inside pocket of his jacket, and unfolded it on the table. It was identical to the one Dorothy had treasured all those years, and which she had with her in her handbag. Francis' eyes flew from the certificate to her face, and found that Dorothy was looking at him with love in her eyes, for the identical certificate told her all she needed, and this was the moment to claim this young man as her son. She opened her handbag and carefully took out her copy of the certificate.

'Look at it, Francis,' she said softly. 'Can't you see it's the same. You're my son, and I'm your mother. Can you ever forgive me for giving you up for adoption?'

His eyes began to shine as the tears backed up behind them.

'Do you mean it? Do you really mean you're my mother? Then of course I can forgive you about the adoption. It doesn't matter, now that I've found you. But ... I wouldn't bother you, really I wouldn't. I just wanted to get to know you, to know you were there. Maybe I could come and see you now and then, could I?'

Dorothy took his hand and squeezed it hard, and he returned the squeeze, as they both sighed deeply with joy and relief.

'Oh Francis,' she said, 'I thought you were gone forever, and I hadn't the courage to try and find you. I was afraid of upsetting your life twice, because you must have been upset when you first found out you were adopted. You have your parents, and probably brothers and sisters, don't you? I was afraid I would be intruding and confusing you, if I suddenly appeared in your life. I built a life without you, thinking that I could never get you back, because I had renounced all claims to you. I wasn't allowed to know the identity of your adoptive parents at the time, and I can only remember the sadness I felt, when they came and took you away from me, a tiny little fellow, one week old.' Her eyes filled up and spilled over.

'It must have been terrible for you.'

'I wasn't more than your age, eighteen, nearly nineteen, and there was no one to turn to. I felt I couldn't tell my aunt who reared me, and I thought I had to give you up. Your father never knew that I was expecting his child, and doesn't know to this day that he has a son.'

'He never knew at all?' asked Francis incredulously.

'I'd only known him a short time when we fell in love, and I've never loved anyone like I loved him. No. I panicked when I found I was pregnant with you, and disappeared out

171

of his life, and over to London, where I was swallowed up in the millions of people there. He was only twenty-two at the time and he was an artist, who intended to live by his work.'

'I am an art student,' said Francis softly. 'I often wondered from whom I had inherited an artistic temperament. I wonder did he succeed as an artist?'

'Let's have our tea,' said Dorothy, 'and I'll tell you as much as I know of him.' They sipped their tea in silence for a few minutes, absorbing all the information they had shared with one another, realising separately that their lives would be changed forever by this meeting. The revelation had been joyful, and huge in terms of emotional experience.

Dorothy resumed. 'Your father was out of Ireland for many years, Francis, but he's back in Dublin at present. In fact he held an exhibition of paintings not long ago, and did very well, according to the newspapers. I visited the exhibition briefly, because I was curious to see his work, but I didn't want to meet him in case it was inappropriate after all these years. He's probably married by now, and I didn't wish to intrude.'

'Where did he hold the exhibition?' Francis asked, interestedly. 'I've been around them all, I think, since I came to Dublin a little while ago.'

'It was in that three-storey gallery in Kilkenny Street, nearly opposite the Dáil, you know, the Irish parliament. He held it there on two floors. He seems to like to work on a broad canvas. I liked them, I must say, even though I only viewed them briefly.'

She did not notice that Francis was looking at her wide-eyed.

'I think I know who you're talking about. Isn't it Frank Donegan? I can't believe this. It is Frank, isn't it?'

It was Dorothy's turn to be amazed.

'Well yes, it is, but do you know him? You say you're not long in Dublin. Did you meet him somewhere?'

'I know him. Yes, I do know him. I held the desk at lunch

hour for him, during the exhibition. Are you saying that the same Frank Donegan is my father, if you are my mother?'

Dorothy sat there, her eyes drinking Francis in. The revelations were coming so fast, one on top of another, that she had to re-gain her composure.

'I held the desk and even sold a picture for him. We got on really well and he was awfully kind to me, paying me for the little I did to help him out. I think I saw you there. Did you come in at lunch hour one day and literally fly around the paintings before slipping out?'

'Yes, I did.'

'I saw you coming in. That's why I thought you were familiar when you came to the restaurant the other night. I was at the desk, talking to someone at the time. You didn't go upstairs, although the exhibition up there was clearly indicated. I wondered about that.'

'I didn't want to delay in case the artist came downstairs, but I was dying to see his work.'

All the time Francis was thinking: should Frank be told about me, and would he accept me as his son? Suddenly he longed for his real father to be Frank Donegan, a man who had been kind to him, and understood his longing to be an artist. His adoptive parents had found it hard to understand that he wanted to study art, and to know that his real father understood this thrust towards painting and sculpture would be wonderful. He had to ask Dorothy more about him.

'Shall I tell Frank about our meeting? And what shall I call you?'

'Oh please call me Dorothy. About Frank ... I can't think clearly just yet. We'll work it out, and whatever we have to do, we'll do. Francis, do you know, is he married, or in a permanent relationship?'

Dorothy's heart missed a beat as she asked Francis this question, so important to her, having loved the man and borne his child.

'No. He's not. I think he has a girlfriend, but she's

younger than he is and I don't think they have any plans for marrying, or anything. He mentioned her in passing. She's a singer, I think.'

'Francis, we'll get to know one another first. And then we'll plan further about Frank.'

A thought struck Francis, so obvious that he stopped short.

'Dorothy, you're not married, are you?'

'No, Francis, I'm not. There's nobody special for me in that way. I could have married a few times, but each time it wasn't right, even though some of the men who asked me would have been easy people to settle down with. I hadn't reached that certain point, myself.'

She found it amazingly comfortable, speaking about herself to this lad, barely a man, whom she hardly knew. Usually she did not mention her feelings to anyone, having perfected the art of covering up her emotions, and here she was, chatting freely with Francis, her son, and liking it. It was a strange yet captivating experience.

'Dorothy, could I ask you about a picture that Frank painted, and which was in the exhibition. Did you see it – you can't have missed it. It wasn't for sale. It was the large picture of the girl running along by the edge of the tide, looking back, sort of ...'

'I did. And I think, and hope it might be a picture of me, painted from memory by Frank, after I left Achill Island, where I met him. We had a wonderful holiday there, and I used to run along the beach ahead of him, thinking the surf would tan my legs quicker. It was a joke between us, and I think that's what I was doing when he first saw me. I'm the girl in the picture, I'm sure of it.'

'I didn't want to ask him about it, but it seemed very precious to him, and, of course, it wasn't for sale. I think he just wanted to have it appreciated by other people. I saw him standing in front of it a few times, when there was no one around.'

174

They smiled at one another and continued to bond, as they sat quietly at their table, absorbing new impressions and recounting old ones. The morning drew on and eventually, two hours had sped by.

'Come into the bar with me for a sandwich, Francis. I don't want to let you go, now that I've found you. Do you have to work today?'

'I do. At four. I don't know what time you have available, but I have until then.'

'Today is a special day in my life, Francis. We have as much time as you want together. Come and tell me about your family and everyone else in your life.'

Francis began again to talk. He told her of his parents and his family life, all about his schooling, and his longing to be an artist. He told her how good his parents had been about agreeing that he study in London, and how hard he had worked for his scholarship; about his girlfriend, Helga, and about his work in the art college with her as his friend. And he told her again about his overwhelming longing to find her. They talked on and on, until at last it was time for Francis to go to work. When they stood up, they were cramped from sitting still for so long, and when they walked around in the leafy sunshine in St Stephen's Green to stretch their legs, she linked him gently. Francis felt proud and excited to have his mother on his arm. He would always remember this park with affection, and he would go to it many a time to recapture this gorgeous feeling of peace and happiness.

When they parted, Dorothy kissed his lovely young face.

'Can you meet me on Saturday morning, you're free in the morning, aren't you? I want to walk down town with my son. Can you meet me at the Dalton at mid-day?'

'I'll be there, waiting for you.'

'Until Saturday, then, the day after tomorrow.'

'Until Saturday.'

Francis saw Dorothy several times over the coming weeks,

getting to know her gradually, without undue stress on either part. Sometimes they had an early morning walk along the strand at Sandymount near Dorothy's home, since her daily work-load awaited her and Francis had to be on duty mid-afternoon. Other times they met down town for a snack at lunchtime and merely walked around together, finding out each other's tastes and enjoying comparisons. Dorothy was thrilled with him, and as soon as he was introduced to Kate and her husband and daughters, a sort of extended family sprang up around him in Ireland.

Francis waited some weeks before he contacted Frank Donegan. His feelings vacillated between hope that Frank would be delighted to find he had a son, and fear that he would be rejected by him. He so dearly wanted Frank and Dorothy to come together for the second time in their lives that he kept putting off contacting Frank out of nervousness. At last his courage came flowing in and suddenly, with the impatience of the young, he rang Frank and asked him to meet him for a pint.

Frank had been seeing Doireann regularly in recent times, and had grown to enjoy and look forward to her company. She stimulated him without involving him in commitment and it was very pleasing, at the end of a day's painting, to clean up and saunter down to meet her for a drink or a meal. A friendship was growing, out of which love might come, and he liked the way it was going. He wondered was he immature in settling for such a young woman's company. Still, he hadn't met anyone besides Doireann with whom he wanted to spend his time.

This evening he was meeting Francis Brentwood, and from the moment Francis walked into the pub in Lower Baggot Street, he could see that something amazing had happened.

'Well, Head, have you won the Lotto, or is that just a light shining out from behind your eyes?'

'Is it so obvious? Well, it's something much better than

money.'

'A lot of things are better than money, but this one must be big.'

'It's big, alright. It is changing my whole life.'

'Seriously?'

'Seriously. I'll order two pints, as I think we're going to need them!'

'Sweet mystery of life, what is it?'

'Frank, I've never told you much about my family, just that we come from Manchester, and that I chose to study in London. Well, it's a little more complicated than that. You see, I was an adopted child, born in London of an Irish mother. The father was Irish too, incidentally.' He stopped for breath, and for courage, as he would shortly have to reveal to Frank who his father was.

'Go on, tell me more.'

'Frank I found her, just a short while ago. I found my birth-mother here in Dublin, quite by coincidence. She booked a table in the restaurant where I'm working and I was able to take the name, contact her, and verify that she is my mother. She's over the moon about it, and so am I.'

The pints came and they gave them their full attention. Then Francis continued: 'There's more to tell you, Frank.'

'Is there now? You've told me more than enough for a start. I want to hear about this woman, your mother. You seem to have taken to her completely, don't you?'

'Frank, I think you know her. I do, really.'

'I know her? I mean, know her well?'

Francis gulped his drink. This was going to be harder to tell. God send me courage, he prayed inwardly. He psyched himself up for the revelation.

'Her name is Dorothy Reynolds.'

'Dorothy Reynolds?'

'Yes, Dorothy Reynolds. It does mean something to you, doesn't it?'

Frank's face flushed and he put down his glass.

'If it's the same Dorothy Reynolds whom I knew a long time ago, it might indeed mean a lot. I never thought I would come across her again. Is she in Dublin, and would fate allow me meet her, do you think?'

'Yes, I'm sure she would meet you.' Francis was so filled with relief that Frank's first reaction was that he wanted to meet Dorothy again, that he found it easier to go on to the next disclosure.

'Frank, Dorothy believes that you are the same Frank Donegan whom she loved long ago in Achill Island, and if that is so, *that you are my father.*'

Frank leant back against the seat for support.

'Dorothy believes that *I'm* your father? Could that be true?'

'She was pregnant when she disappeared out of your life, and I was born in London where she lived when she left Dublin. Look at me Frank. I'm not unlike either of you, am I? And I'd gladly have the blood test needed to establish it medically, if you wanted it.'

'Francis. Is Dorothy married, or involved with someone? I have to know.'

'No, no. She isn't. She doesn't have anyone special.' The words tumbled out of Francis.

Frank was silent for a while, cradling his glass and thinking back on his life.

'Francis, I never knew that Dorothy became pregnant as a result of our time together in Achill. Stupid of me not to have realised that that was why she vanished. A penniless artist might not have been delighted by the news in those days, when there wasn't much in the way of support for single mothers. But I can tell you this: I think it would be wonderful to have a son of my own, particularly someone I'm fond of already, and who shares my passion for art. Now what would you think of me as a father?'

'Too good to be true! My adoptive parents have been wonderful to me. They can't share my interest in living as an artist, but it doesn't matter. They know I've found my mother, and they'll meet her soon when we go over to introduce Dorothy to them. Maybe, by that time, you'll be coming too? I suppose it's too much to hope for?'

'We'll sort it out as soon as possible, Francis.'

The bar man passed by.

'Same again, Sir?'

Frank nodded.

'Francis, I have to begin by meeting Dorothy. I would never rest again, if all this weren't cleared up and acknowledged. It's a lot to absorb at one time, and you'll have to act as go-between. You see, I never forgot Dorothy. She's the girl running along the sand in the picture you liked in the exhibition. I painted it to hold the memory of her, just after she vanished from my life, so that I would have something of her. And now, it looks as if I may have her son and mine, in you.'

'When do you want to meet Dorothy, Frank?'

'She's the lady in the situation, and so it must be on her terms if it's to go right from the beginning.'

Vera Nolan clenched her teeth, stood up and dragged one foot forward and balanced. She had taken her first step, unaided and in secret. If positive thinking could make her walk again, walk again she would. She stood there, shaking with excitement, safe in her precious morning hour of seclusion, then she slid back her foot and re-gained her chair. She had walked! Tomorrow she would try two steps.

She switched on her computer and slipped in the copy of Dan's disk, on which she was working. Dorothy was holding the original for safety, in case Vera accidentally erased any of Dan's work. She had carefuly edited ten pages since she started, and she was quite elated at the thought of participating in creative writing at last. There was great achievement for her in what she was doing, and as she studied the text, the sensation of having lost everything emotionally was gradually receding, with the subsequent effect of her confidence trickling back. How good Brian had been in building this garden room and other facilities for her. It was *her* space, not to be invaded by anyone, even her family, who dropped in regularly to see her, but always asked first if they could come in. It meant that if she were working on the book, she could leave her papers undisturbed, and go off happily to the front of the house in her electric wheelchair.

Vera applied herself once more to the typescript. The early chapters had nothing of her in it. It caught the reader's attention from the start and introduced the main character, who was so like Dan in personality that sometimes she had to snigger to herself with amusement. When she had edited about four thousand words, and was satisfied that the text was free-flowing and grammatically correct, she allowed herself to read a chapter further on in the typescript.

The nerve of Dan Devereux! Men should be banished from the face of the earth! Similar recommendations filled her mind, as she read of his meeting with an older woman in a writer's circle, and of his plan to seduce her, gently, firmly and delightfully, leaving the full consent to her at all times. Each time she came to a description of herself, in the role of Sally, she ate up the words. She had to admit that she came out of it rather well, and this man certainly could appreciate an older woman. She read on, and she became ever firmer in her resolve that this book should be written and submitted to a publisher.

Dan Devereux worked extremely hard that summer, organising his property for the raising of ostriches, and the development of a herd of deer. If these projects were successful, he would buy adjoining land and extend his interests, taking on staff and turning the place into a type of theme park. He rose early every morning and flung himself into the work, enjoying it for its own sake, and moving out from home more, as he came in contact with others.

Preparations were well ahead for the coming Wexford

Opera Festival, which would take place at the end of October and run for about two weeks, one of the big items on the European musical calendar, and when he was approached with a request to work as a volunteer, he agreed. As he had an interest in classsical music, and quite enjoyed opera, he was quickly absorbed into the corps of voluntary workers, and he soon found himself painting scenery and helping generally. It was just what he needed, organised sociability, and he began to look forward to his evenings in Wexford town after a day of activity at 'The Shallows'. The company of Wexford residents and incoming professionals was stimulating, but he tended not to stay late, as he had to be up so early each morning, running the various enterprises at 'The Shallows'. There would be plenty of opportunities for socialising at the time of the Festival, he told himself, although his guilt regarding Vera still impeded his social skills.

12

Vᴇʀᴀ ᴡᴏʀᴋᴇᴅ steadily on her two projects, learning to walk again, and editing Dan's typescript. She confided to her physiotherapist about her achievement in walking one step, and they worked out a plan of exercises for her to follow, so that each day she gritted her teeth and achieved a fraction more movement, until, after some weeks, she could actually walk a few steps unaided. Now was the time to call in Brian and show him what she was made of. He was so overcome with delight for her that he wept openly, and Vera began to understand better this man she had married in such a business-like way. Before meeting Dan Devereux she had never understood any man, much less her own husband, but when she saw real love flow from Brian as he rejoiced with her in her success, she began to draw closer to him with every new step she achieved. It was a humbling and greatly enriching experience for Vera, one she could never have anticipated, and Dorothy was the only other person with whom she shared this secret about the walking.

The same was happening with her writing project. Flushed with success about her efforts to walk again, she applied herself daily to the novel, and she achieved a good first draft, up to the point where Dan had stopped. It was as if she had taken someone else's cleverly knitted garment, and finished it off correctly, washing, pressing and joining it deftly, neatly inserting fasteners or buttons at the points in the design of the creator of the garment, and giving the piece the finish it deserved. It now read fluently and well, without losing the originality of Devereux's style. She would have to plan with Dorothy as to how it should be completed, and with whose help.

While she worked on it, Vera suffered occasional deep stabs of disappointment. When the story touched her too closely, she would sit back, let the tears gather in her eyes and flow over, and then allow her grief subside in its own time. By this means, what she had lost would lessen in reality, and what she had gained would re-surface. It was her own form of therapy, and it was working for her. On very good days she fantasised about the book being a hit or even a bestseller, or being adapted for television, or imagined that it would be translated into other languages, but she was not without humour since her affair with Dan, and she would eventually giggle at these premature and somewhat ludicrous notions.

Dorothy kept in touch with Vera faithfully, coming over a couple of hours each week, and working closely with her, and Brian was enormously impressed with her dedication.

'Dorothy,' he said one evening as she was preparing to leave. 'I'll never plumb the depths of your goodness. Your own life is more than full, and still you find time to help Vera speed up her recovery process. The writing project is helping her in walking again, and the walking is helping her persevere with the writing. It's amazing to watch it all going on. How and why do you do it?'

'Brian, don't be silly. You know I enjoy working with Vera, and anyway I have spare time, in spite of what you think about my workaholic ways. Don't you know I'm on a daily diet of monkey gland extract?'

'Seriously though, Dorothy, I really wonder at your goodness. Imagine, I didn't even know Vera was computer literate, and here she is further on in the use of the computer than I am.'

'She's doing fine, and that's all that matters. Do you know, Brian, we're like two schoolgirls producing a magazine in a garden shed!'

'Dorothy, my dear, we've come to the point where I can't make any further progress. We've got to bring someone in on this book, otherwise the story will collapse, and there are several chapters still to be written. What'll we do about it?' It was

Vera facing up to the next challenge.

Dorothy was pleased with Vera's practical approach, and her lack of literary notions.

'Leave it for the present, Vera, and I'll come up with something. I'll hit on some solution, see if I don't.'

'What a relief! I'll take a break from it for the moment, and I just know that you'll be back to me on it with some miracle solution.'

'Hopefully. I'll rack my brains about it. We can't do less than a good job on it, that's the priority. Print me up a full copy and I'll take it away with me.'

Dorothy was seeing Francis regularly, and he told her that he had told Frank Donegan everything, and that Frank very much wanted to meet her. She hugged the knowledge to her heart, and mentally prepared herself for what could be the greatest development in her life yet. Yes, she would meet Frank, in the company of Francis. It was both thrilling and somewhat frightening, but a current of life was running through her, which had been blocked all these years, and she rejoiced at the sensation.

It remained for Frank to do something important before he arranged to meet Dorothy. He would have to see Doireann, and tell her all about his new-found 'family', and he needed to do it soon. He phoned her to see if she was back from a singing tour of Northern Ireland, and having made contact, arranged to meet her.

When Doireann arrived at their usual meeting place, it was Frank, this time, who looked as if lights had been lit behind his eyes. She noticed it immediately.

'Come on, you've good news of some kind,' she said. 'Have you been commissioned to paint the crowned heads of Europe?'

'Better than that.'

'You'll have to tell me.'

'It's difficult, but when I do, I hope you'll understand

right away.'

'You've come into possession of the Coca-Cola formula?'

'Ah stop! No, it's better again.'

'Ah, come on, tell me. Out with it. I'll need my lager in front of me by the look of things. Order one for me, will you?'

'Oh sorry Doireann, my manners have gone out the window with excitement.' He ordered her drink and took a mouthful of his pint to steady his nerves. Then he began to tell her the sequence of events involving Dorothy and Francis, ending with, 'I haven't met Dorothy yet Doireann. I just wanted to tell you all about it first.'

'Take your time, Frank. I want to hear it all.'

'Well, this lad has found his mother and from what she has told him, it seems that I'm his father. He has a copy of his birth certificate, and so has his mother, and in fact, he's not unlike me in many ways. Wants to live by his art, as well. You can understand how I'm knocked out by all this, can't you, Doireann?'

Doireann took his hand and held it.

'Oh Frank, I'm so delighted for you. I'm so glad for you. It was such a waste of a good man for you to be on your own!'

'You're happy for me, Doireann? You've been such a friend, and I've enjoyed you so much, all the chats and the company. It's been lovely, and thank you for being you. It's a marvellous feeling that I may have a family of my own, although I've yet to meet Dorothy, as I said. Francis is arranging that for me, and I might as well tell you that I'm as nervous as a kitten about it.'

'Don't worry, Frank. It will be all right, you'll see. You've been a good friend to me too, and now I'm losing you, but that's the way it has to be. Let's drink to your happiness and my career. That's happiness to me.'

They clinked their glasses and Doireann looked at him and smiled.

'Don't order another for me this evening, Frank. One will do. We'll surely meet again, sometime, and then we'll have the other drink.' She bent over and kissed him warmly, and before he could say a word she had slipped out into the summer evening, among the crowds standing around, and on to her own life.

Francis waited until both Dorothy and Frank were ready for the occasion, and then he arranged for dinner in a good place at Dun Laoghaire, the neighbourhood he always regarded as special, because he felt it had welcomed him into Ireland. Dorothy had told him of a restaurant near the seafront, known in the trade for its atmosphere, soft and glowing, with pink napery, and a wonderful seafood menu. He went out in advance and made a reservation, asking the Head Waiter to give them special attention. Dorothy had entrusted him with the arrangements, and had handed him a cheque which would cover the evening, so that, as 'man of the night', he would feel in charge all the way.

The evening arranged for the dinner grew near, and Dorothy had never experienced such intense excitement in her life. She fussed around for days organising herself, had her hair done in a youthful style and she bought a dusty pink silk dress, beautifully cut and deceptively simple. A pair of wildly expensive court shoes completed the outfit. She took a day away from the desk to get ready, doing her manicure in the morning and slipping into a relaxing bath during the afternoon, when she had taken a long walk along Sandymount strand to feel fit and have colour in her cheeks.

Dorothy wanted Francis to feel proud of his new mother, and she wanted Frank Donegan to like her, at least! She felt like a young girl going to her first formal occasion and before she slipped into her new clothes, she did something she hadn't done for a long time. She knelt down by her bed and said some silent fervent prayers, asking for peace and happiness, so that the evening would be a great success.

If the mirror was telling the truth, Dorothy was looking wonderful, and with a slight spray of her favourite perfume, she was ready. Throwing a light coat over her arm, she went downstairs to wait for the taxi to arrive with Frank and Francis. When the door bell rang, she put down the coat and crossed the hall to answer it, her heart swelling with excitement. She opened it and there stood the man she had once loved, and the son she had borne him. The three of them stood in the hall smiling, and studying one another, and then they impulsively joined hands in a tripartite squeeze of joy that lasted some moments. Breaking free at last, Frank Donegan broke the silence.

'You haven't lost it! The spirit of Dorothy. You haven't lost it!'

Francis stood there beaming in his role of controller of emotions, and then they all went across to Dorothy's sitting-room where she served a drink to settle them down. It had all the potential for a wonderful evening.

Eight months later, spring broke through in Dublin once more. It was one of those late springs, when nothing seems to be happening in nature until April arrives, and then one day, within twenty-four hours, leaves unfurl, and within a week blossoms begin to open up as if photographed on a slow camera.

It seemed a long time to Dorothy since that evening in Dun Laoghaire. It had been so wonderful for all three of them, so *right*, that she could not have described it to anyone. She could only tell Kate that it was a 'meant-to-be' evening, their code for those events in life over which no one has final control. Asked what any of them had either drunk or eaten, none of them could have replied accurately, and the night had gradually unrolled, assuming its own pace. Frank had found it difficult to take his eyes off Dorothy, and in the company of the two new men in her life she had been radiant. At the close of the night Francis said, 'I've ordered two taxis for us! I want to go home on my own and leave you two to get to know one another.'

They had laughed, and hugged him before he swung out of the restaurant, having looked after everything, and acquired the status of a fully grown man in his own eyes and theirs.

When they reached Dorothy's home, they sent the taxi away, and it was a magic moment for both Frank and Dorothy, as they stood in her sitting-room, their arms around one another, their mouths seeking the first kiss since that time so long ago. As Dorothy melted into his embrace, all the defences she had built against the world were washed away, and two people found again the love they thought was gone forever.

These were happy months, but there still remained the finishing of the novel, and Dorothy was proceeding slowly and carefully on this. Dorothy figured that Frank would be the right person to write the ending of the story, and Vera could then continue with the work of editing. She talked out her plan with Frank and then with Vera, and they both agreed. Frank liked the plot when he read the typescript, and felt that he could solve the murder mystery deftly. He was busy painting the Midlands, travelling up and down frequently, and he said it was just the occupation he needed for the evenings.

Brian might well guess that Vera was the star of the novel, but he was unlikely to throw over his new happiness by letting it trouble him. Dorothy knew Brian Nolan very well, in the way that women know men with whom they have worked closely without any sexual relationship, in a way that sometimes wives do not know their husbands, and she knew that she could trust Brian in this matter.

The strands of the various lives seemed to be weaving themselves into a fabric, and Dorothy enjoyed watching these developments. The new threesome moved into a house looking across Dublin Bay from Sandymount, but she kept on her town house as office premises. And she continued to work successfully with Abdul Shamir, who had had to renounce his dreams of a relationship of some kind with her. Allah was wiser than he, he thought, when Dorothy told him her news.

She and Frank were married quietly, with just Francis, Vera, Brian, Kate and her husband at the ceremony, and the honeymoon was spent on Achill Island, where Dorothy and Frank walked the strand at Keel with arms around one another once more, as they had done as young lovers, and as Vera had done with Dan Devereux at Garrycloe.

When Frank had finished the book, he pronounced himself satisfied, knowing from his own world of painting that there are no short cuts to the arts, and being able to judge the quality of his own work. A summary of it was sent to a few publishers, which led to a contract for publication. Vera's spirits soared. This was the final impetus she needed in her efforts to walk, and she made great progress in a short time, determined to be fully mobile by the time the novel would be launched. She was even unintentionally funny about the arrangements, once they became a reality, reading the contract with care, and deciding that she should publish under her own name and strike a good deal while she was at it. Her old personality was resurfacing, and Dorothy was vastly amused at her business-like approach to 'her' book. The recipients of miracles are often surprisingly calm, and Vera now had no further qualms about Dan Devereux coming for his pound of flesh.

The book was a success, and on the day of the launch Vera Nolan walked unaided into the room to a wave of applause. During the proceedings a courier arrived bringing a parcel containing a box with a Waterford silversmith's stamp on it, and inside was a finely-carved silver brooch, featuring a man and a woman on a motorcycle, the woman leaning forwards, her arms around the man's waist. Tucked into the lid was a small card, blank except for the words:

Congratulations! From one good loser to another!